THE
MOTO BOYS

DISCOVER CHAOS AT SILVER MINES

RANDOLPH NORDYKE

Published by Kinetic Digital Publishers

www.kineticdigitalpublishers.com

Table of Contents

CHAPTER 1

Trouble at The Diner

It was a beautiful, cold fall morning in Clear Springs. The sun was shining brightly, but make no mistake - fall had come to Clear Springs. A small mountain town nestled in the heart of Montana, Clear Springs was perched 35 miles away from the closest larger town with a supermarket. The population of Clear Springs was 2,483 people.

The town was very close-knit and very patriotic. The town had two beautiful churches, a small but well-stocked grocery store, and a modest motel that catered mostly to summer vacationers. A busy hardware store served as a vital hub for the community, kept busy by the many families who made their living as farmers, ranchers, or in construction.

The next small town was about 10 miles to the east, named Whispering Pines. It had a population of 812 people and was slowly growing. The people in Whispering Pines did not want their town to grow too quickly. They did, however, want to have their own grocery store soon - particularly when the weather got ridiculously cold and icy. Sheriff Don Weldon also oversaw Whispering Pines, as Clear Springs was such a small and peaceful town that it never truly needed its own dedicated sheriff.

Nobody really remembered Clear Springs ever having trouble - until the Wednesday before the Fall Parade. Logan, who had recently gotten his license, drove himself and Gage to dinner at the diner. Almost everyone at the diner knew each other, but today, two large men sat at the counter—strangers to the small town. Gage and Logan had never seen them before.

Something seemed off with these two guys; at times, they were loud, and at other times, they were whispering to each other. There was an unspoken rule at the diner—no one used their phones. In fact, they were put away, allowing people to enjoy real conversations over lunch or dinner. There was actually a poster on the glass door when entering the diner:

⅏⅏⅏

"We appreciate your business, and we appreciate everyone staying off your phones inside our diner. If you need to answer the phone, please take it outside. Thank you!"

⅏⅏⅏

Bob answered his cell while sitting at the counter, immediately drawing the attention of everyone sitting near him. Heads turned as people glanced over to see who was daring to break the unspoken rule. To make matters worse, he was loud—and had the speakerphone on.

Meanwhile, Mary, a longtime server at the Clear Springs Diner for over ten years, did her best to be polite, attempting to engage the men in conversation.

"My name is Bob, and this is my older brother Larry," said Bob. "People where I came from called me Big Bad Bob, and my brother is Large Larry," he added, saying it so loud that anyone around them could easily hear them.

"Oh, I haven't seen you before," said Mary, a little uneasy from the conversation. "Yeah, we're not from around here, but we kind of like it here," said Larry.

"We're hungry and thirsty," said Bob. "Mary, let's start with a couple of beers." Mary smiled, but under her breath to herself…

"Oh, great … just what you need."

Several minutes later, as Mary was walking by, Bob grabbed a few French fries off a plate she was taking to another customer.

"What do you think you are doing," yelled Mary. "Didn't your mother teach you any lessons?" Both Bob and Larry laughed, "Oh, what's the big deal, yelled Bob…it's a couple of fries?"

By then, everyone around the tables went quiet. This wasn't a dive bar- people around Clear Springs weren't used to this kind of crap!

"Hey, I tell you what," said Bob, "whoever that plate belonged to, I will give them a couple of *my* fries."

Clearly, Bob and Larry found this situation hilarious. But Mary was carrying Knox Hartley's plate, a big, muscular rancher, who was watching this whole thing unfold. Knox was there having dinner with his family and children, and clearly, he was not amused! Slowly, he rose and walked to Bob and Larry.

"So you like my French fries, do you?" asked Knox. Whatever possessed you to think it was okay to grab food off someone else's plate, let alone MY plate," replied Knox.

Bob and Larry stood up and got right in Knox's face, but Knox did not back down.

Boys, "I am a retired Navy Seal," said Knox. I wouldn't think twice of thumping you two clowns, so I would suggest you back off…do not test my patience!

Bob and Larry moved a step closer to Knox, and Knox did not back up…nor did he flinch.

"Oh, we're really scared," said Larry.

Sheriff Walden and Deputy Colton walked inside the door. Mary had told the owner, who then called the Sheriff. They were only about a minute out when the call came, said Sheriff. "We don't have trouble in our town…where you two are from anyways, and I need to see your IDs."

"Ok, we'll just leave Sheriff," said Larry. Both Bob and Larry grabbed their coats, and threw down some money on the counter.

"No, I don't want you to leave quite yet," said Sheriff. "I said give me your ID's, NOW," he repeated himself and this time a little louder.

"Really, Sheriff, we're sorry, we'll just be on our way," said Bob to defuse the situation. Sheriff was a patient man, but now his patience had worn thin.

"Ok Deputy, let's put them in cuffs, I am done asking," Sheriff said, turning to his partner.

"Ok, ok, pardon me Sheriff," said Larry. Clearly, the Sheriff did not want to cuff them, he just wanted them out of Boise.

Finally, they both pulled their IDs out. Their IDs revealed their background, clearly, they both were from a small mountain area outside of Boise, "What brings you two to Clear Springs?" asked the Sheriff. By now, he had them moved to the back of the Diner, so that people would go back to eating their dinner.

"WHY ARE YOU HERE?" asked Sheriff Weldon, his voice firm. "Hey, we heard Clear Springs is a beautiful little town, and we just wanted to come, check it out," said Bob.

"Deputy, go call in their IDs and see what you find," said Sheriff. Deputy Colton went to the truck, and called the Sheriff's office in Boise.

"Where are you staying when you are here, said Deputy Colton. "With our Aunt outside of town," said Larry. "We promise…no more trouble, Sheriff," said Bob. Deputy Colton came back several minutes later, pulled the Sheriff aside, so Bob and Larry couldn't hear what he was saying.

"I spoke with the Sheriff's office in Boise," said Deputy Colton, known as DC to the Sheriff. "Larry spent 6 months in lock-up for aggravated assault, and Bob was charged last year with grand theft, but the charges didn't hold…the Deputy I spoke to said they believed both Bob and Larry intimidated the witness, but they couldn't prove it."

The Sheriff thought for a minute. "Well, we don't have enough to hold them or lock them up, so let's get them out of here, said Sheriff.

When the Sheriff came back and handed them back their IDs, "I took care of your bill… that's the good news," said the Sheriff.

"The bad news is you're not coming back into this diner. Since you didn't finish your beers, you can go ahead and go as soon as you've had dinner!"

After about 20 minutes, they got up to walk out. Bob was staring at the Sheriff, but Larry grabbed Bob by the arm, saying, "let's get the hell out of here!"

As these two lefts, the patrons of the diner all kind of quietly clapped after they were out the door and out of sight.

"Remember, said Bob to his brother, "We want people to get over us…we got bigger plans." Larry just smiled at his brother, and they both laughed as they walked down to their lifted 2018 4-wheel drive Chevy truck. To no one's surprise, their truck was loud and obnoxious. And true to form, they raced the motor and drove away, burning rubber.

Up the mountain were two ghost towns, that were almost impossible to reach; many years back, there once was a bridge called *Eagles Crossing* that led the way to these two extinct towns. Now, however, you had to navigate down a steep embankment, wheelie through the deep stream, and climb up the other side.

It wasn't easy, but each of the boys who made up the motocross boys could make it across. From there, you had to trek several miles through dense forest trails before tackling one final, steep hill. Eventually, you could see the back side of Silver.

Clear Springs had a beautiful mountain fragrance, and when the boys rode, there was the fragrance of 2 stroke exhaust! Nothing like 2 stroke exhaust for people who ride!

From drawings that were found regarding Silver Mines, once upon a time, it was quite the town! It was a very wealthy town back in the day, thriving on gold and silver mining. A large Wells Fargo bank stood at its center, alongside a hotel perched on the second story of the saloon. The town also had a jail, a schoolhouse, a church, and a bustling livery stable.

There was an area just outside of Silver Mines, with at least 5 or 6 beautiful, huge mansions, three on each side of the dirt road. The road was lined with huge oak trees. It was called Silver Mines Estates. These mansions are apparently beautiful.

Supposedly, the richest families of Silver Mines built these massive homes, and spared no expense in building these mansions. But the area was hit hard by smallpox in the 1880s, which led to fortunes won, and fortunes lost in Silver Mines!

Several online articles claimed that the mansions in Silver Mines Estates were haunted. These articles talked about doors slamming, loud screaming in the walls, chandeliers swaying, Imagine, experiencing this in these mansions!

But getting to Silver Mines, even for these guys, would be extremely difficult. The Dalton boys, Logan and Gage, were told, don't even try to reach Silver Mines!

"You guys are never going up to Silver Mines," said the boys' father, Jacob Dalton. He made his point crystal clear—Jacob would do anything for his sons, and in return, they never wanted to disappoint their pops.

There were two articles online about the Silver Mines Estate mansions being haunted.

There was another way to reach Silver Mines, but it involved going the long long way around. The journey required a four-wheel-drive vehicle like the Can-Am Defender or Maverick— even a sturdy four- wheel-drive truck, like the one the Sheriff drove, wouldn't be able to handle the terrain.

Even then, it would be extremely hard getting into this ghost town; you always had a chance of running out of gas, too! You could get a helicopter up there if ever there was a life and death emergency, but the trees up on the mountain would make getting a chopper up to Silver Mines very risky.

Perhaps the best part of Clear Springs town was the "Clear Springs Diner" that had the best pancakes, hamburgers, and chicken fried steak. It was always busy. There was also a great little bakery that supplied all the pastries for the diner, always offering fresh coffee and even a classic soda bar. The smell of fresh apple pie drifted from the bakery, adding to the cozy ambiance of the small community.

Today was a special day because of the fall parade, and everyone from Clear Springs and Whispering Pines showed up to either cheer on the floats, horses, or the one fire engine. Sheriff Weldon and Deputy Colton also participated in the parade, their patrol car flashing its lights as it rolled through town.

It was the only time anyone in town remembers the Sheriff turning on the lights, as Clear Springs is a town where everyone looks out for everyone else, and is considered a "very quiet town."

The Dalton family transformed their flat trailer into a cool miniature farm. The two Dalton boys rode along with their riding buddies, joined by the two girls from next door, Chloe and Emma. The other boys on the trailer, Bobby, Charley, and Travis, were good motocross riders.

The best rider among the boys was Gage, closely followed by his older brother, Logan. Gage was just two weeks away from turning 15, while Logan was already 16. In fact, several older men in the neighborhood who used to race that Gage could probably be a successful motocross racer told Gage.

But it would be too hard on the family to travel to race tracks, and Gage knew it. All the boys were just grateful to have bikes to ride after chores were done on the weekend. To avoid disturbing the families of Clear Springs, the boys set up their track two valleys over. They even coasted their bikes to and from the area to keep noise to a minimum.

The two Dalton boys were close, but very different in interests. Gage was creative, and was a good drummer and guitar player. Gage was smart, but not the greatest student. He could not wait for school to end so he could either ride or play music.

Logan had a passion for computers and could take apart and reassemble a desktop in no time. He also loved writing code— something that made no sense to anyone else in the Dalton family. School came too easy for Logan, and planned on finishing high school early.

The way Logan rode his KTM 300 EXC was methodical yet very fast. Gage, on the other hand, had a more carefree riding style, pulling off tricks and maneuvers that none of the other boys could match, like "wheel tap" into bumps, and could triple jumps, go over logs without putting a foot down.

On the track they set up, Gage was so much faster than the other boys, with the exception of his brother Logan. Every now and then, Logan could keep up, but when Gage wanted to turn up the heat, no one else stood a chance! Bobby was the next fastest rider, but he also took chances. He got hurt quite often trying to keep up with Gage or Logan.

Bobby was also the loudest when they weren't riding. He had trouble paying attention in class, and last year was held back because of his grades. But when he strapped on his helmet, he could fly.

Charlie was a good rider, was very good in narrow trails, and was a very technical rider. Charlie was also a quiet boy, very good student, and was an only child. His father was a professor at the Community College in Kalispell; Charlie's parents were not crazy about him riding, but they knew he was a good rider, who really looked up to Logan and Gage.

Charlie preferred to just listen. He thought Bobby was funny, which encouraged Bobby to be a little squirrelly at times.

Travis, nearly 15 years old, was the youngest of the riders. He looked up to the Dalton boys, always listened intently, and was eager to join every ride. When they weren't tearing up the trails, he and Gage spent their time playing music together.

They even talked Travis into playing some music with them; Gage taught him how to do basic drumming, and when the three of them got together, it was Gage and Charlie on guitar, Travis on the drums.

All in all, the "motocross boys" were good kids, respectful, and were well liked by the families in Clear Springs.

By the weekend, most people in Clear Springs had almost forgotten about the incident at the diner. It was time for the fall parade! Gage and Logan were super excited to join in on the fun. Bobby, Charlie, Travis, and the two girls next door, Emmy and Chloe, made their way onto the float they had made, with their dad, Jacob, driving the tractor. They had a stereo set up on the trailer, blasting country music.

Colorful floats decorated with autumn flowers and pumpkins paraded down the street, accompanied by the upbeat rhythm of the school marching band. It was a small band, but it was perfect for the town of Clear Springs. The town was alive with laughter and cheers as families and friends gathered to watch the parade!

After the parade, all the friends, and their families, gather at town's favorite diner, where they grabbed burgers and milkshakes, their all-time favorite thing to do. The kids sat together laughing and chatting while the parents gathered at their own table. These families are close-knit, always ready to help out when someone was in need. That was the heart of Clear Springs – families who looked out for each other.

As evening descended, the Dalton family headed home. The boys unhooked the trailer, and all the friends pitched in to help unload. Gage went to feed the two horses and their family donkey.

About the time, they were done, Margie Dalton went inside the house.

But within seconds, she was yelling at the top of her lungs.

"Jacob…WE'VE BEEN ROBBED!" Margie's voice was frantic as she called for Jacob and the boys to come into the house.

Jacob tried to stay calm, but his tone and demeanor showed him upset, and VERY pissed. It was clear they had gotten his nice watch, and a lot of Margie's jewelry as well, some of which was worth a considerable amount of money.

The worst part…they broke open his gun case, and stole three guns…Jacob's Browning X-Bolt 2Pro SPR, an X-Bolt 2 Western Hunter, and his Smith & Wesson X-Frame pistol.

"How could this happen, he said to himself. In this town???"

Logan went to the back door, and saw that was pried open. "Dad, check this out, this is where they broke in, the back door is completely jacked"! Jacob was quiet by that time. "You have to be shitting me," said Jacob, who very seldom cursed. Margie was crying. It was such a violation of privacy, realizing that someone had been inside their home, stealing very expensive items from the family!

Jacob immediately called the Sheriff, and before he could tell utter what they found missing, Sheriff said, "Jacob, three other families were also robbed…you need to come down here immediately!"

"Jacob, what is it?" said Margie. He put the phone down. "Three other families were also robbed, I have to go see the Sheriff," said Jacob.

"You boys stay here with your mom, right now, she needs the support." The boys were not familiar with this kind of situation in Clear Springs, it was new for them. It was supposed to be a safe, peaceful place.

"Dad, it has to be two guys who just came into town," exclaimed Gage!! Normally, Dalton boys never interrupted their dad, nor would they talk to him in a loud tone, but deep down, Jacob knew his family was extremely upset, mad, and not to mention…. scared.

Jacob nodded and agreed… "Well, right now let me go meet with the Sheriff and see if we can put the pieces together, I will be back in a bit," said Jacob. Logan called all the guys, including Chloe and Emma, and told them to be at the track at 10 am. "I have an idea," said Logan eagerly.

CHAPTER 2

Born Are the Moto Boys

Sunday morning, the Dalton boys sat down at breakfast with mom and dad to hear how the meeting went with the Sheriff the night before. "Dad, who does the Sheriff think robbed us and the other families?" asked Gage in an excited yet still scared tone.

Jacob Dalton stared down at his breakfast, slowly raising his eyes to look at his family. Margie Dalton chose to just listen, but clearly, she was still both upset AND mad about finding their house robbed.

"The Sheriff has a plan," said Jacob, "And believe it or not, it might include you boys and the boys you ride with. Next Saturday, we all meet at the Sheriff's office.

I've already talked to all of the parents."

"C'mon dad, tell us what the plan is, and why are we waiting till next Saturday to meet," said Gage! I thought we were meeting tonight," said Logan with a quizzed look on his face. "Not yet boys, the Sheriff and I meet again in a half hour…you guys get you're riding in this morning. I'll fill you in tonight!"

Margie was clearly not in a good mood, but chose not to say anything, at least not right now. Jacob stood up, gave his wife a kiss on her forehead. "Right now, you all just have to trust me for now," said Jacob. "And the Sheriff!"

The boys looked at each other with a small smile…they knew their lives might get a LOT more exciting. At least they hoped!

"Let's go, Logan," said Gage, super excited. "Hey Dad, I think we both know who ripped us off and stole from us, and I hope we get to kick their butts" said Logan. Jacob looked over at his boys and shook his head, "Do you remember that in this country, you're innocent until proven guilty," said Jacob. "But WHOEVER it is….I want to kick their butts too!"

"Be careful, boys," said Margie. That was something their mom said every time they went out riding.

The track on this Sunday was in perfect condition from the rain earlier in the week. That meant the dirt was tacky, loamy with deep berms. Both Logan and Gage study the Supercross riders that they saw every Saturday on TV. Gage tried to emulate the riding of Jett Lawrence. Eli Tomac and Chase Sexton. Logan's favorite rider was Chase Sexton.

The KTM 300s were great for both motocross and for trail riding. The backwoods and trails were amazing, but the boys were never allowed to go in the woods by themselves. This is Montana, which means grizzly bears, mountain lions, and other dangerous, large animals.

One of the things that made Gage such an amazing rider was his ability to stand up in many of the corners, as well as get back on the pigs and get his weight back as quickly as he could coming out of the corners. Charlie and Travis tried to copy Gages 'amazing riding style. Bobby had his own style.

The girls next door, Emmy and Chloe, tried to ride every time the boys did, and they were always welcome. Both Gage and Logan enjoyed teaching the girls how to ride, and they were improving every time they rode. Their dad had bought the girls used KTM 150 enduro bikes, and they fit the girls like a glove!

Logan was almost as fast as his younger brother, and today, both Logan and Gage were about the same in terms of speed. You could tell that today all of the boys were riding with a lot more determination. Definitely, the break-ins that happened with the Dalton family were on their mind.

Logan signaled for all the guys to stop on the top of one of the hills, and when everyone had turned their bikes off, he told them the meeting with the Sheriff wasn't happening until next Saturday night.

"What's gonna happen, Logan," said Travis. Are we going to help the Sheriff get those guys? I mean, hey, it's exciting, but we're just kids!!" Gage could tell that when Travis brought that up, it kind of deflated the group's excitement…. "Yeah, we're just kids"…you could feel it was going thru their minds.

"Hey, we don't yet, but I'm sure Sheriff thought this through, so let's just be on time next Saturday, and be ready to listen to what he has to say," said Logan. The other boys trusted the Dalton brothers, particularly Logan. He was wise beyond his years and had great leader ship skills for a kid that was 16 years of age.

It did not make sense to any of the boys as to why the Sheriff was waiting until next Saturday to meet; didn't the Sheriff understand the robbers could be long gone by next Saturday??

"Let's race another 10 minutes, and if any of you can catch Gage or myself I'll buy you a hamburger next time we go to the diner," said Logan. Well, race they did, but by the time 10 minutes were up, Gage and Logan were a half lap ahead of the rest of the boys, with Gage turning up the heat on his older brother. "Dang what got into you…you were flying out there," said Logan to his brother. Gage just smiled…and started coasting and pushing his bike back home. Fortunately, it was mostly downhill going back home.

The next weekend could not come fast enough. All of the boys were instructed by their parents NOT to talk about the upcoming meeting with anyone. Bobby, however, again not following instructions, leaked it out to a couple of boys at school. This leak got back to Logan.

Both Logan and Gage went up to Bobby at his school locker, and grabbed Bobby by the collar. "Bobby, what were you told," said Logan in a muffled but mad tone. Bobby looked over his shoulder to make sure no one was listening. "You were told not to talk about it, and that is exactly what you did….now I have to tell the Sheriff you leaked the info, and you might not be included, said Logan!"

Bobby immediately started crying. "Logan, I am so sorry, please, please, don't kick me out," begged Bobby. "PLEASE"!!

Logan grabbed his collar a little tighter, "that was dumb Bobby, you could have screwed everything up! Do not mess with me or the other boys!" You've been warned," said Logan.

Logan and Gage walked off, and Logan said quietly to his brother, "Ok,

I think we nipped that in the bud," he'll be fine!"

Finally! Saturday late afternoon was here, and it was time for everyone to meet with the Sheriff. Logan and Gage were ALWAYS hungry, but this time they could barely eat their dinner.

"Hey Logan, I can see the girls and their dad coming up the walkway. Let them in," said Margie, as she started to clear the dinner plates. Emmy and Chloe's dad, Bill, was a successful contractor, like Jacob. His specialty was cement. Bill and Jacob often referred jobs back and forth to each other. The girls' mom, Cindy, was a stay at home mom, as was Margie, and both families were close friends. They two families looked out for each other.

Cindy came over, mainly to keep Margie company with last night's events fresh in everyone's minds. "Okay, guys," we will wait here with bated breath to hear what is going to happen," said Cindy.

"What does 'bated breath 'mean, Mom," said Chloe. "It means we can't wait to hear about Sheriff Weldon's plan, said Cindy, now get going!"

As they entered the station, there were about 20 to 25 chairs set up. No one was sitting yet, as everyone was milling around. Charlie, Bobby, and Travis's dad was there, and a few new faces up near where the Sheriff was about to start the meeting.

"Ok, everyone lets grab seats' said Sheriff Weldon. As you can imagine, Sheriff Weldon was a big guy with a deep voice. "I appreciate everyone being here, and I will tell you, we've never had this kind of problem here. In fact, I really sometimes wondered why I had the job of being Sheriff in this great town! And now I know why," said the Sheriff as he looked out over the group.

"If this were just a small time grab and steal, we would not be meeting like this, but it turns out this is much more serious, and it now has my full time attention," said Sheriff. Everyone just looked around at each other, wondering what Sheriff Weldon was about to say.

"I want to introduce you to a new addition to our team, who happens to be Deputy Colton's nephew," said the Sheriff. His name is Johnny, but for you guys, call him 'DJ 'for Deputy Johnny. He is a retired Army Ranger, and over the last two days, he snuck up to Silver Mines and found a group of at least four people, two of who he believes were this Bob and Larry that caused the problems at the diner last week"!

Deputy Colton smiled and put his arm around his nephew, "Hey, boys, DJ is in fantastic shape, he's smart and is a quick learner," said Deputy Colton. So, you boys need to teach him how to ride."

The boys all looked at each other a little confused. Deputy Colton had clearly gotten ahead of himself.

Sheriff Weldon interrupted Deputy Colton, "Well, we have a lot to tell you boys. What you don't know yet is, we cleared our plan with your dads, and you guys will be working with DJ," said the Sheriff. "You guys will be deputized as Cadets. The only one carrying a gun will be DJ…. he will be your leader."

"So, guys, I took a few days and went up to Silver Mines," said DJ.

"After the Sheriff, DC, and myself met, we decided to find out if the stolen goods could be held up in Silver Mines, or, were they on a truck never to be seen again."

The boys were dead quiet, just looking at each other. "Look, let's be honest, there is no way we are going to put you in a position of danger," said Sheriff. "What we need you to do is help train DJ to ride like you guys, and second, accompany him up the mountain."

"You boys have a big responsibility. This is much more than just trying to get stolen goods back, said the Sheriff. "More than anything, we need to protect against FUTURE problems, because we now have a major glaring problem on our hands…for BOTH towns," said Deputy Colton.

"You boys, if you agree to help us, I'm calling you the MOTO BOYS, said the Sheriff. "What do you boys think? Can you help our towns out…we need you," asked the Sheriff?

All of the boys nodded their heads YES, without saying a word.

"But…you have to pass the tests that we made. And you have to go thru additional training that both DJ, Deputy Colton, and myself, have developed for you boys," said Sheriff Weldon. "It may sound fun, and perhaps it will be, but it will be a lot of work too. But, we do need your help"!

"The first test is the riding test we made, which is to get across the river and up the bank where the bridge got washed out in less than 45 seconds," said the Sheriff. Now I know you boys can all do that, because I've seen you do it. The other test…. you have to run up the embankment in less than 2 minutes," said the Sheriff.

"You parents need to understand…. again, we are not putting the boys in danger," said Sheriff. "It's up to DJ to keep them safe, and out of harm way…but having them get up the mountain is no small deal"!

"I do not know if all of you can do it, or just a few can do it, but we need to know you are physically fit," said DJ. If you can't, then I'll help you get fit, and get fit in a hurry!" The boys looked at each other with kind of a puzzled look.

"This way we know you can handle anything that can come our way," said DJ. "We will all carry a small pack on our bike in the event we have to spend the night, and…carrying food. We have to be ready for anything and everything," said DJ.

"One more thing," said the Sheriff. "Our department will pay for all the bike parts you need, and all of your gear needed for these trips." Hopefully, we won't have to make many of these trips, but based on what DJ has learned, we have a real problem on our hands," said Sheriff Weldon.

"What do you think, boys… are you still in?," asked DC?"

"Emmy and Chloe, I want you to train with DJ and the boys," said the Sheriff. "But we're not ready to have you on any trips yet into Silver Mines. But we want you to test and be ready…just in case!"

Bill looked down at his daughters with a wry smile, and shook his head in approval. The girls certainly understood, and they both knew they were not ready for an adventure like this. They were just proud to be included in the group.

"Okay boys, we start training tomorrow," said DJ. I'll meet you up at your track at 10 am, and we need to train also on trial riding, because there are a LOT of trails, streams, logs…even animals like Grizzlies we have to watch out for on the way to Silver Mines!"

"I kind of figured you boys would help us and DJ out," said Sheriff with a grin.

"Hey, can we get sweatshirts saying 'MOTO BOYS'," asked Travis. All of the boys looked at each other, and Logan said one word…."NO"! And that was that, no one asked that question again!

But all of the boys were super excited to be a part of helping the Sheriff…and their new friend DJ!

"Let's go eat," said the Sheriff. "I'm buying"!

CHAPTER 3

Ten-Hut

They had a lot to talk about at dinner. Chloe fixed her spot next to Logan, who was steering most of the conversation.

"We have to show up big tomorrow," said Gage while observing the group. We will all pass the riding test, but we have got to nail the running test too, including you girls," he added, looking pointedly at the girls.

DJ joined the group, having been listening to Logan and admiring his leadership. "So, you boys think you can teach a 26-year-old guy like me to ride?" DJ teased. The guys laughed, knowing DJ would catch on quickly.

On Sunday, the day after meeting with the Sheriff, training started at 9 a.m. Everyone was amped up for today, and everyone's parents were there to watch their boys, not to mention Emmy and Chloe, who were included in all training.

Gage and Logan were primarily training DJ, and he was totally impressed with the boys' riding, particularly Gage's. "Holy crap, Gage! How did you learn to ride like that," DJ exclaimed? Gage beamed with pride, including his brother.

"If you can just get me to half that fast, I'll be good, but let's see if you can keep up with me on the hill run, boys," laughed DJ. Theparents were filming their kids riding, and several of these parents had not seen their boys ride lately.

That was not the case with the Dalton boys or girls because their parents often watched them ride. Particularly, the girls' dad…he was an involved and proud dad that loved watching them ride. He knew that his oldest girl, Chloe, liked Logan, but he also knew that Logan was a respectful young man who appreciated their friendship. They had never kissed to his knowledge, it was just a matter of time.

They continued riding for about another hour, and with each passing lap, DJ was getting better and better. He fell several times, but every time, he got up with a smile on his face, and started back up with no complaints.

Meeting at the top of the hill on the track, Logan reminded them they needed training riding in the forest, too. "Guys, let's follow Gage into the forest, and leave room between each person," said Logan. About that time, Sheriff Weldon showed up to ask the boys a question. "Hey guys…and gals, after you do your training in the woods, let's put your bikes in the back of your parent's trucks, and then, let's take the test," asked Sheriff? "Can you handle it?"

"Heck, ya we can handle it," said Gage. "Right after a quick trip into the woods, okay? It will only take 30 minutes, Sheriff."

Starting with Gage, all of the riders, including DJ, rode really hard thru the woods. Both Gage and Logan were really fast on the way in, then led by Charlie, Bobby and then Travis. Poor Travis felt a little dejected that DJ was already faster than he was, but you could understand how, since Travis was the youngest, and his parents constantly telling him to be careful.

It was surprising that Travis's parents would even let him train for this kind of an adventure, but they also didn't have the heart to not let him be included. He was a good kid, and…the Sheriff made it clear that each and every one of them was an important part of their team.

Sheriff also reminded Travis's and Charlie's parents, again, that the boys were not there to be in harm's way. They were there to help get DJ up the mountain, and out of harm's way. And they could always pull the plug on the boys being involved!

After the trip thru the woods, it was off to Eagle Crossing. It had rained two days before, so the dirt was in perfect condition at the ravine. The Sheriff told everyone before they started part 1 of their test, that once they all got to the other side at the top, he would motion for them to ride down to the stream, and one by one, they would run up the hill.

"Okay, Gage, I am sure you don't need me to time you for this part of the test, but why don't you lead them off, "said the Sheriff. All the boys cheered on Gage, and even though he was trying to have a serious look on his face, he was also smiling under his helmet.

Margie, the boy's mom, had never seen them ride on this part. All she could think about is how STEEP the hill both down and up the other side were. "I am not sure I can watch Jacob," said Margie. "Piece of cake, honey…piece of cake," said Jacob.

And like a flash, Gage went down the hill, wheeled through the stream, and up the other side he did it…In 26 seconds!!

"Well… doesn't that set the tone?" asked the Sheriff. Both Bobby and Travis said at the same time, 'What was the time, Sheriff?" When he said "26 seconds," they all started laughing.

"Let's go guys," yelled Gage. All of them knew they were going to get up the other side, although the girls were a little worried about making it up the hill for both tests!

Next was Logan, who made it up in 29 seconds, also a very fast time. Next to go up was Charlie, who took 39 seconds, then Bobby…at 38 seconds, and then Travis, who was 42 seconds.

"Sheriff I want to wait," said Emma. I am afraid I will go back down. Bill, the girls' dad, said "honey, if you want, I will be up on the other side to catch you…I think it would be good for you to try." Emmy thought about it, and then the Sheriff said "hey Emmy think about it for a bit…no pressure."

Chloe, on the other hand, was anxious to try. "Chloe, Choe, Chloe," chanted the boys. Hey girl, we got you; you can do it," said DJ. Do you want to go before me or after me?"

"You go," said Chloe. And like that, DJ headed down the hill and through the stream. He didn't wheelie thru the water like Gage or Logan, but he hit the other side of the hill with plenty of speed. He was probably a gear too high when he started up, but he quickly went down to second and towards the top, went into first gear.

DJ made it!! And everyone cheered for him! It was easy to see how well he fit into the team, and what a great leader he was for the boys. And like that, before the boys could start cheering for Chloe, she was going down the hill, standing up the way Logan had taught her. She hit the stream with her weight back and then hit the hill with great speed.

About halfway up, she shifted to 1st gear, keeping her weight forward, and as she got towards the top, she started to stall…but she kept the motor going by feathering her clutch. Logan and DJ grabbed her handlebars and pulled her up!

Everyone cheered Chloe, and she wore a wide smile on her face. Her mom almost couldn't watch, but she was proud! After all, she had never been up a hill that big, and she did it on a 150!

Now was time for the second part. They had 2 minutes to make it back up the hill. So down the hill went Gage, sliding down the hill. He gathered himself, and everyone at the top was already cheering him on. "On your mark, get set, go," yelled the Sheriff from the top of the hill.

All the parents, riders…everyone was cheering him on. "45 seconds,"

yelled the Sheriff. He was well more than halfway up the hill, but everyone knew the hardest part was the last 1/3rd of the hill. Gage stopped for a second, then continued up.

"Cmon, dude, you got this," yelled DJ. He stopped again…."1:15," said the Sheriff. Gage had about 15 more feet, and he sprinted up the rest. "YESSSS!" yelled all the guys. "1:30" was your time, Gage…great job," exclaimed the Sheriff.

One by one, the boys, including Chloe, went down the hill. The only one of the boys that went over the minute mark was Travis (2:07), with Chloe doing the climb in 2:35. But she finished, and the Sheriff, and her parents, couldn't be any prouder!

DJ was the fastest at the hill climb at 56 seconds. He wasn't even breathing hard at the top, and the boys thought it was hilarious. "Okay, everyone, let's meet at the diner, the department is buying lunch, and we have some things to go over," said Deputy Colton. "So, go home, grab a quick shower, and meet there in half an hour," said the Sheriff. "Let's see how quick you can get over there…oh, and also, parents are expected to," said the Sheriff.

As the parents, along with the boys…girls too, pulled in, everyone met the 30-minute mark, except Bobby. He was almost 10 minutes late. As they got to where the boys were sitting, the Sheriff came up to Bobby and said to both Bobby and his parents, "Bobby, why are you guys late?" asked the Sheriff. He kept his voice down so not to embarrass any of them, but nevertheless, he was asking in a serious tone.

"Sorry, Sheriff, it was my fault," said Bobby's mom. "I decided to change, and I just didn't think it was going to be a problem." Bobby was embarrassed, but Sheriff liked that Bobby did not make excuses or try to get mad at his mom.

"Well… it's important to the team that everyone is on time, I am sure you can understand that, yes?" The Sheriff made his point, and said with a smile, "okay, let's all eat"!

Bobby's dad spoke up, "Hey Sheriff, we understand, and we appreciate this opportunity for Bobby…the last thing we want to do is screw it up!"

After everyone finished eating. DJ stood up and addressed the group, "Alright, everyone, the Sheriff has some updates for us. Pay attention," he said. Deputy Colton nodded.

"Okay, everyone," said the Sheriff as he looked at the group, in front, in back, and to his sides, "We found out two more families were robbed yesterday!"

It was clear that the Sheriff was upset. "You won't believe this," he continued. "This family and their neighbors drove all the way to

Billings because their 13-yeard old daughter is undergoing chemo." The Sheriff paused for a second; he was clearly pissed and emotional about what had happened.

"They were gone all day; her husband came home from work and found they, AND the neighbors, had been robbed."

"Now, just how did the thieves know to rob them," asked the Sheriff. "Plus, the neighbors getting robbed, on that particular day?! I don't believe in those kind of coincidences," said Sheriff. "I think we have a much bigger problem on our hands than we first thought!"

"So…we are moving up your trip to this coming Friday, instead of Saturday," said the Sheriff. "The weather we believe will get better, and we believe they may be expecting us at some point…and the weekend would be more likely," said the Sheriff. "So hopefully, we can surprise them by a day."

"We have jackets, gloves, undergarments, and new backpacks for all of you. Be sure to ride with your backpack on to get used to it," said Deputy Colton.

"When you ride, we also believe DJ should be leading the pack, as he is the only one with a gun, and he has proven himself as a good enough rider," said the Sheriff.

Truth be told, the boys were happy to have DJ take the lead. "Hey, guys, said DJ, let's review the map and create our game plan." It would be good for your parents to know what the general plan is, too."

The parents stepped back, giving DJ room to spread out the map, but you could see they were as eager as the riders to know the plan. "Alright, here we go," DJ said with determination. "Burn this plan into your heads, boys."

CHAPTER 4

Silver Mines

As the boys leaned over the map, eyes wide with anticipation, the "Road to Silver ines" came to life in front of them. It was a mashup of Google Maps and DJ's own scribble notes, a perfect blend of tech and boots-on-the-ground insight. The girls, being

smaller, wormed their way in front so they were also able to see what was going on too; they were a part of the team too!

"Okay, guys, we are all going to get dropped at Eagle Crossing-EC for short to save gas. We ride out at 7 am. Sharp, so get a full night's sleep and have everything prepped tonight," said DJ.

As the group scanned the map, one thing jumped out: the number of buildings scattered across the ghost town of Silver Mines. It clearly had the boy's attention, but he brought their eyes right back to Eagle Crossing, now known as 'EC'.

"Hey guys, I'll talk about Silver Mines in a few minutes, but know this," said DJ. This trip is going to be a tough one, and as much as we plan, we have to be ready for anything!" He had the group's full attention, including the parents.

"Once we get to the top of the mountain, you can see the backside of Silver Mines, "said DJ. "That is why you can't see Silver Mines on this map. At the top of the mountain, everything changes!"

The mix of emotions on the parents' faces was palpable. At first, there was pride, excitement, and the fact that their boys were now a part of something significant. The excitement was real! Their sons' inclusion in this endeavor was a big achievement, but beneath a new fear crept in: this wasn't just a fun ride through the woods.

Even though the boys weren't supposed to come close to any of the criminals…they knew all along… it could be a possibility!

"Be suited up except for your helmets when you get out of the truck," said DJ. "Then get your bikes started, warm them up, put on your backpacks, helmets, and gloves, and Gage will lead us across EC. From there, we ride about 1/4 mile to the first forest edge. It gets dark in there, so have your lights on the whole time!"

"When I get to the other side of Eagles Crossing, I'll wait for everyone to get across," said Gage. "Getting across Eagle will be one of the hardest parts, I believe, and everyone can do this…so we got this, guys.”

DJ brought their attention to the far edge of forest #1. One thing the boys did not know was that there were two forests, two hills, another mile of relatively flat trails, and the final hill before they got to the edge of Tumbleweed.

“As we get through forest #1, now known as ‘#1’, let’s make sure everyone’s gear is good, and that everyone is doing ok,” said DJ. “Then comes the second forest, steep, longer, harder, and darker.” It should take about 45 minutes to get through #2.”

“The first hill is not difficult, guys, but the second climb is tough and long,” said DJ. This is why back in the day, no wagon, horses, or cars could make this way of getting to Silver Mines…you’d have to go the LONG way around, which is undoubtedly what these guys did to reach Silver Mines.”

“The very last hill is steep, but pretty short,” said DJ. “We’ll hide our bikes halfway up and hike the rest. No doubt by the time you get up to the back side of Silver Mines, you’ll be tired, and that’s where it gets real,” said DJ, as he looked out over all of the boys.

The Sheriff leaned in to get closer to the conversation, eyes scanning the nearby dinner booths. “Hey DJ, we can’t be too careful, I don’t know some of the people walking by, so bring your voice down,” said the Sheriff. So, you boys…and girls…listen very carefully…okay, DJ, carry on!”

“Silver Mines was quite the town once upon a time,” said DJ. “It had everything a town back in the 1860s would ever have. Once we park our bikes, about halfway up this last hill, we’ll walk up to the edge of the town from the back side.”

The boys, AND their parents, were fixated on the map. They were all looking at the pictures DJ had taken of Tumbleweed for the first time. “Goal number one is to find our place to hang out and rest,” said DJ.

Then we decide if we are going to turn and burn, or…are we spending the night," said DJ.

"When we come up the hill, we are kind of in the middle of the town, on the back side," said DJ. We come right up next to the Wells Fargo office, which has two rooms, I think. Next door is the barber shop, and next door to that is the General Store…this is where we will hang out," said DJ.

"Now, lean in, guys," said DJ even quieter. Right next door to the General Store is the Saloon and hotel, which is where they were last time and where they should still be. We should be able to hear them through the walls!"

"But…we have to be super quiet…what we referred to in the Rangers as Stealth Mode," said DJ. No one talks to one another, otherwise, our cover is blown. No flashlights, and watch every single step you take!!"

The Sheriff glanced around the group. Bobby and Travis looked a bit uneasy. "One sec, DJ," said the Sheriff. If ANY of you are having second thoughts, it's okay, you can back out and not worry about disappointing any of us!"

The boys all took a second to look at each other, and Gage said, "I'm all in." One by one, every hand went up- including Bobby's and Travis's. By that point, no matter how scared or worried any of the boys were, they were not going to disappoint the team, the Sheriff, or their parents.

"Okay, continuing on," said DJ… "take a good look at the map, just so you guys get the lay of the land." DJ waited to see if they had any questions. "You guys have to watch for my signals and what I say, once we are in Silver Mines."

The boys wondered how they would hear the signals when they had to be so quiet, but they were all fixated on what DJ was saying.

"Why are you wanting to be right next door, asked Logan. So, we can hear what they are planning?" Before DJ answered, Deputy Colton got close to the table and opened up a large bag.

"Exactly, we want to hear what they are planning, said DJ. Like the Sheriff said, they have bigger robberies, which means bigger problems, we believe they are planning." DC

"Now, DJ will have the radio and the earbuds," said Deputy Colton. "Logan, you are second in command!" Chloe was standing right next to Logan, and you again could tell just how proud she was of the boys… particularly Logan!

"I want you guys to burn this diagram into your heads," said DJ. We will get to the General Store from the back. "Fortunately, or unfortunately…. it will be near full moon. That is good for visibility. Bad for staying hidden."

Logan could tell the boys that they were suddenly feeling a little scared and down. "Hey guys, we got this!!' I want you to remember, the Sheriff wouldn't put us in any danger deliberately. Remember, we are there to assist in getting DJ up the mountain," said Logan a little too loudly.

"Okay, guys, go home and get some sleep, said the Sheriff! "Do not, I repeat, do not say a word to anybody!!" Everyone put a hand in here, on 3, .1,2,3…. "Moto Boys"!

You could tell everyone was tired and completely spent. They needed sleep!

The next morning came fast, but the boys and DJ were ready before 7 am. They were well prepared, and they made it up thru both Forest 1 without any issues. About 5 minutes into Forest 2, DJ held his hand up to have them stop. "Take your helmets off, grab some water and a snack," said DJ. It was dark inside the forest with the headlights off.

"Listen to how eery it sounds in here," said DJ. Nobody said a word, they all just took it in. Finally, time to move on, and they maintained almost perfect time getting thru the upper edge of Forest 2. After about another 5 minutes thru the meadow, you could finally, but just barely, see the backside of Silver Mines.

They kept riding on until they got to the corner where they decided they would hide the bikes. After they hid their bikes, grabbed a drink, they came out of the trees and could see fully the backside of of Silver Mines.

"From here on, we whisper, "said DJ. "We get up the top of the hill, keep your head down, I will take a look to the front, then we go to our spot, in the back door, and hide behind the counter in the General Store. Any questions?"

No one had any questions, and up the hill they went. All of the boys had the conditioning to make it up with no problem. DJ went right to the front, peered around the corner, and came right back up.

"Okay they are out doing bar-b-que," said DJ. Let's stay close to the edge of the buildings, watch your step, it's getting dark." Within 30 seconds, they were at the back door of the General Store. The door was surprisingly un-locked, and the door was a little creaky, but they all made it in, and got down below the counter.

They kept riding on until they got to the corner where they decided they would hide the bikes. After they hid their bikes, grabbed a drink, they came out of the trees and could see fully the backside of of Silver Mines.

"From here on, we whisper, "said DJ. "We get up the top of the hill, keep your head down, I will take a look to the front, then we go to our spot, in the back door, and hide behind the counter in the General Store. Any questions?"

No one had any questions, and up the hill they went. All of the boys had the conditioning to make it up with no problem. DJ went right to the front, peered around the corner, and came right back up.

"Okay they are out doing bar-b-que," said DJ. Let's stay close to the edge of the buildings, watch your step, it's getting dark." Within 30 seconds, they were at the back door of the General Store. The door was surprisingly un-locked, and the door was a little creaky, but they all made it in, and got down below the counter.

DJ went to the front window to observe, and called Logan over. "Okay, I am going to go out in a bit, and go over to the church to look for stolen goods, "said DJ. "I will give you the satellite two way, and we only whisper from here on, okay?"

Logan just shook his head yes, and they watched DJ slip out the back door. To not be seen, he went down the bank and went over to the back side of the church and went in the back door. "Come in Logan, can you hear me," whispered DJ. "Yeah I can hear you," said Logan. So far, they are staying still.

"Logan, how does DJ know the stolen goods are in the church," asked Gage. "He doesn't for sure," said Logan. "But it's more than likely!"

"You cannot believe what I found here, "said DJ. "So, so many stolen things here, from guns to watches and bracelets, "said DJ. I am going to try and take what I can for now!"

"DJ, HIDE," said Logan in a very loud whisper. "They're coming over!!" DJ acknowledged and hid in the back room out of site.

"Hey Max, so what I'm thinking is we move this over the houses so NO ONE can find these goods tomorrow, "said one of the guys. DJ had no prior knowledge of hearing these guys from before. But hearing the one guy called Max…well, no confusing him now.

"Okay, I like this idea," said Max in a thick deep Russian voice. "We get you guys paid next week!" DJ tried to peer around the corner, but decided it was too risky, not to mention, the floor could creak and what a disaster that would be.

"Okay for now, let's leave things alone," said Max. I want to get back and eat your American tri-tip!"

DJ waited for them to go out the door, and then went over to where the jewelry was. He realized one of them left their beer on the table, and he suddenly heard them open the door. He moved as fast as he could to get behind the door. It was an extremely close call!

He assumed the guy walking back in was Bob, based on the boy's description of him. Suddenly, the floor creaked where DJ was, and Bob hesitated to look around. He started to look around, but thought better of it, and he walked out the door with his beer.

DJ continued grab as much jewelry as he could in his back pack, and then it was time to get back to the boys!

CHAPTER 5

A HELLA RIDE HOME

DJ slipped quietly out the back door, made his way to the edge of the hill, and sprinted to the GS, where the boys were all getting ready to sleep.

"OK, listen, guys," said DJ, catching his breath. "You're not even going to believe what I've just heard!" When DJ told them the plans, their eyes grew wide, thinking whether they would be a part of going to the Silver Mines Mansions, or, as they now called it, "SE" for Silver Estates.

"I think I've got a plan, but I have to talk about it with the Sheriff," said DJ.

"C'mon, DJ, "said Bobby a little too loudly. The boys hushed him all at the same time, which made Bobby feel bad.

"Sorry, sorry," Bobby mumbled.

"Hey, all good, but now, I need you all to sleep, I have first watch, then Logan, then Gage, then Charlie," said DJ.

The boys were exhausted, and within minutes they drifted off to sleep. "Come in, Sheriff," said DJ over the radio. "I'm here, DJ," said Sheriff. "What's going on? I am here with the Daltons and Deputy Colton at the diner," said the Sheriff. "Let me get to a quieter place to talk."

When DJ told Sheriff about the whole incident, and that he had some or most of the jewelry, his reaction was "Ok, fantastic, at least Margie is gonna be thrilled, but focus on getting back okay!" said the Sheriff.

"I assume you're leaving early in the morning to get back, the weather looks like it could be nasty"!

"That's the plan, the boys are exhausted and sleeping now," said DJ. The offenders were now outside the saloon, where they had a BBQ grill, and were starting to get loud. It woke the boys up, except for Travis, who was absolutely worn out and in a deep sleep.

"Hey guys, drink up, and cheers to our new hauls, the last couple weeks, with MUCH more to come," shouted Bob in excitement.

Meanwhile, Larry wandered the boardwalk, his boots clunking on the wooden planks. DJ crouched at the edge of a window, ducked quickly out of sight. He could have gotten caught very easily!!

"I thought about it, I think we should take load number one tomorrow," said Max. "This will save us a lot of time, not waiting till the last minute."

It was clear that Max was the leader, and whatever he said, the other guys snapped to and did! Now midnight, DJ needed a couple of hours sleep. Logan did not get much sleep, but he knew he could last a few hours.

Two hours later, DJ woke up, and he let Gage take the lead. But Gage was out! So, DJ took the lead again, and Logan was already asleep at the change of guard. Not exactly what would be expected in the Army, but DJ was okay with it.

Now, at 2 am, the hooligans next door were finally asleep. DJ had to go pee, so he quietly went out the door, and did his business. Outside it so quiet and serene, with the exception of wolves howling; he was pretty sure there was a mountain lion howling too, none of which were a concern to DJ. The full moon was now gone, and the stars were incredible.

Charlie's turn to take watch came next, and he was more than ready. The thing about Charlie is that he followed directions perfectly and was a great listener.

"Okay, I got this," said Charlie. DJ realized that as it got close to 4 a.m., it was too risky to have anyone by the front window, so he had Charlie take a watch from where he had been sleeping.

DJ knew it was going to be a long day ahead, with rain and lightning on the horizon. Charlie also drifted off to sleep during his watch, which DJ had planned on happening. He knew that the gang next door would keep sleeping since they were up till about 2 am.

At about 7 am, DJ roused the boys, reminding them to be quiet. "There's no point in staying here any longer, let's get back to Clear Springs," said DJ in a whispered tone. Just five minutes and we are out."

The boys got ready and filed out the door one by one, waiting for DJ to close the door.

Around the backside came Bob! No doubt the boys were scared out of their minds!

Bob was as surprised to see the boys, as the boys were to see him. He was obviously there to do his morning "business."

"Hey, what are you guys doing up here," asked Bob in a quizzical deep voice. He sounded half asleep. The boys realized they were right in front of one of the criminals…the dude they called "Big Bad Bob"!

DJ quickly interjected. "Hey there, I'm taking the boys on an adventure, and we're about to head back. The weather is going to get bad," said DJ. DJ had a big smile on his face, trying to be as friendly as possible.

"You guys were sleeping next door," asked Bob. "What time did you get in?" "Oh man, we got in really late, hope we didn't wake you up," said DJ. Logan thought quick, the longer we were there, it was not going to be good.

"Hey, DJ, if we don't get to a bathroom soon, I'm going right here," said Logan.

"Well, we better get going…duty calls," said DJ. Bob raised his hand as to say, "yeah, I get it that is what I came out here to do," said Bob. Obviously, Bob had not caught on yet that DJ and the boys knew that they were criminals, so he too was trying to be cool, calm and collected.

By the time the boys started to walk away, Max was walking over to the school. Max didn't catch on quite yet that Bob was talking to someone. DJ knew it was time to get out of there.

"Have a great day," said DJ as he was walking away now at a fast pace. Now Max heard someone else talking to Bob, and was completely confused. He figured he would talk to Bob once he got back to the saloon.

"BOB STOP THEM…WE'VE BEEN ROBBED"
yelled Max!

DJ looked straight ahead, without flinching. "Don't turn around, run down the hill, boys," said DJ, now much louder and stronger.

"Hey, stop, get back here," Bob and Max yelled. By this point, all four of the offenders were at the top of the mountain. DJ turned around for a second and yelled back up, "Hey, these boys have to go to the bathroom bad…gotta go," acting like he didn't understand what Max was saying!

Maybe stealing back the jewelry wasn't a good idea, thought DJ to himself.

Larry started down the hill, but no way he was going to catch up to the boys and DJ. "DJ, are they gonna come after us in their Can-Am?" asked Charlie. DJ was keeping one eye back on those guys at the top, and Larry was now down the hill and on flat ground. DJ could tell he was struggling to chase at this point.

"Guys, you can go to the bathroom inside #2, let's get the bikes started," said DJ. Everyone's bike started right up, except for Bobby's.

It would not start! These Yamahas are usually easy to start! "Okay, come hold my bike, Bobby," said Logan, who also was scared! "Let me try."

By then, Bob had caught up to Larry, and they could tell something was preventing the boys from all taking off, so they picked up his pace…as best he could! DJ had to think fast. Was he going to hold them off with his gun? Was he going to fight them? He knew he could handle one, but maybe not both…but he didn't want to get to that situation!

DJ figured Max was telling them to chase us. Now the focus was back on getting Bobby's bike started. "Try pushing it," said Gage. Bobby turned off Gage's bike, put the kickstand down, and joined the push.

Finally, Bobby's bike started to flubber and finally, it started. By now, Larry and Bob were about 100 yards away, and closing fast! "Let's go, Boys," yelled DJ!

And off they went!! It was about 2 miles until they started on the upper side of #2. Once they got about 300 yards down the path, he turned around to see where they were on the trail. Both Larry and Bob gave them the bird. …They gave up the chase!

Bob and Larry made it back to the top of the backside of town. "I'm beyond pissed," said Max.

"They got some good stuff, but now, this place is blown. Let's get it over to the big house, and just hope they never saw those mansions."

No one else dared say a word. They just waited for Max to finish ranting. "I am hoping it was just a group of stupid boys who think they got lucky. I want you guys to find out why they showed up here, and…we'll steal it back from their parents"!!

DJ laughed out loud as he rode away, realizing Bob and Larry no doubt had a tough time climbing that hill, particularly as it was getting wetter. DJ also knew they had a rough ride home, with wet trails, more water to cross, and maybe lightning ahead.

DJ motioned them to stop before they got into #2, so they could finally do their business and grab a quick snack. "Five minutes, boys," said DJ. They noticed elk in the meadow and saw several deer just on the edge of the woods. No bear, at least yet.

Gage led them in this time. "Show the boys technique, but don't go too fast," said Logan. They could feel the rain coming through the woods, and the trail was slick. Part of the trail had a crown to it, and if they fell or went off the single trail, they had a long way to slide down. They had to keep their "eye on the prize," as Logan called it…and the prize was staying on the trail!

A loud crack of lightning came thundering down, making the woods much brighter, scaring the crap out of Bobby….and down went Bobby! Both he and the bike slid down the hill.

That would scare anyone…including DJ!

"Bobby, are you okay?" yelled DJ. "Get me up!" cried Bobby. DJ was scared for Bobby…imagining sliding down a hill, and being so dark down deep in the woods. That would scare the crap out of anyone…including him!

"Breathe, Bobby, breathe…and grab the rope I'm throwing down to you. I am pulling you up to your bike," said DJ. Then, you are going to take the second rope. We'll pull you up first, then your bike," said DJ.

"Put the rope around your waist, Bobby," said Logan. As they pulled Bobby up to his bike, DJ threw down the second rope, and Bobby tied the rope around the back tire. If nothing else, it showed the boys that they can get out of just about any jam!

Finally, Bobby was back up, muddy, wet, and extremely tired. "Okay, catch your breath, get some water, let's clean off your grips and gloves," said DJ. "You are good, all good"! DJ smiled at him to try and loosen him up. He knew Bobby had the crap scared out of him.

"Sorry, guys," said Bobby, who was still crying. "Hey, all good, catch your breath, and we will get going," said Gage. Off to the left side, they saw a black bear, and being from Montana, the boys were used to seeing black bears. They knew they would not approach the boys.

The lightning became stronger and louder. The rain slowed just a tad, but the weather was no doubt getting worse!

"Okay, let's go," said DJ. This set them back 25 minutes, but DJ figured they would have some small setbacks along the way.

After about 12 minutes of trail riding, they got up to the stream with the waterfall; the water was flowing much faster! No doubt it was getting harder to ride! The boys kept both feet on the ground, except Logan and Gage, who stood up almost the whole way, riding on the single-track trail.

Getting across the stream this time required another set of skills, and only Gage, Logan, and maybe DJ could make it. Gage blew across the water, as did Logan. DJ made it, but barely. Bobby, Travis, and Charlie put up their kickstands and welcomed Gage and Logan to ride their bikes across the fast-moving stream!

Finally, they got to the lower end of #2 Forest. The weather, definitely getting worse, with lightening, thunder, with rain coming down harder! Not stopping, they took off down the hill to get to the upper edge of #1 Forest. It was now close to 11:30 in the morning.

The upper edge of #1 was now visible. They were riding beautiful green meadows, and the scenery was incredible. All of a sudden, Logan slammed on his brakes, hand in the air, and in front of them was a massive mountain lion staring back at the boys!!

DJ carefully moved his bike past the boys on the single-track trail to get to the front. No easy task with how slippery the trail had become! He pulled out his massive flashlight and his P320 pistol. He had zero plans on shooting this massive animal; he just wanted to scare it away. He fired his pistol in the air, and this huge cat only moved a little closer.

No one said a word…they knew enough to let DJ do his thing. DJ fired another shot a little closer to the lion, and this time, it ran off. They waited to make sure the cat was really gone, and DJ fired one more shot to be sure.

By now, it was a little past noon, and they could see the woods coming up in front of them. Given that they had made it through #2, they felt it would be no time at all, and they would be home. The thunder and lightning were getting stronger, as was the rain…all of a sudden, it felt like a deluge of rain!

"Let's go, let me lead," said DJ. They took off, and about a hundred yards in front of them was a fast-running stream that was just a small stream on the way up the mountain.

There was no way they would be able to ride their bikes back and forth without someone getting washed down the stream!! They still had to get across the super-wet log!

The water was moving fast, but not super deep. "DJ, the only way is to hit it pretty fast," said Gage. "Let me go first." Gage gunned the motor, let out the clutch, moved his weight as far back as he could, and went flying across. It was a massive amount of water that came up.

"DJ, holy crap, the lion is back," yelled Gage, as DJ was about to get across!! DJ gunned his motor, and as he was going across, his weight was not back far enough, and the front end slid out. He sprang to his feet no worse for wear, except his bruised ego, and…he was completely wet.

He kept his eye on the cat, which barely moved with DJ making a commotion getting across the stream. "Gage, be ready to help them, I am staying right here watching this lion," said DJ. Gage moved into position and told them all "keep your weight back…ALLLL the way back," said DJ to the boys, almost yelling at this point.

DJ loaded more bullets in his pistol and never took his eye off the lion, which was about 30 yards away. The cat was now crouching down, which really worried DJ. Again, he did not want to shoot this lion, but he would if he had to protect the boys!

Bobby made it across, which was great because after his fall, he needed a win. Next was Charlie, who made it across but also slid out as he came across, but was not hurt. He quickly got up to make room for Travis and Logan.

Travis got ready to go, he rode like a pro. Logan could tell he was crying in his helmet. No doubt he was thinking about the fast-moving water, and a damn mountain lion to boot! "Look, you got this," said Logan very calmly. "You know what to do, you did the training…you got this"!! Travis gunned the throttle, put his weight back, and he looked like a pro going across! In fact, he was almost as smooth as Gage!

Logan went across even more easily than Gage. "Why don't we start looking for rocks to throw…and start yelling?" said Logan! DJ, without looking anywhere but in front of him, said, "Good idea!" The boys grabbed any rocks they could and started yelling.

"Okay, get back," said DJ. "You guys throw rocks, I'm going to shoot towards his feet, and see if I can scare her off, I'm guessing she has babies around here." DJ squeezed the trigger slowly, aiming towards the huge cat, being careful to not hit it.

"BAM"! The pistol was louder because the bikes were off, and the cat ONLY moved closer!! "Okay, start your bikes," said DJ. I hope the bikes scare the cat…no way I am shooting and putting this lion down"! The boys understood, because they were now pretty freaked out.

All they could think is, Thank God DJ was there!!

The boys revved their engines until Logan told them, "Hey, we also have to conserve gas!" DJ started revving his bike and letting his clutch out as if he was going to hit the lion, and FINALLY, the lion ran off! That took a half hour, and they had not even hit #1 yet!

"Okay, you guys, keep an eye on the trail," said DJ. "Gage, Logan, and I will watch for the lion or any other scary creature that can come our way"!

They took off. It was now 1:30 p.m.; DJ hated that they were out in the open with thunder and lightning, but they couldn't help it. Deep down, DJ knew, no matter what came next, somehow, they'd make it home.

CHAPTER 6

This Was Not a Good Idea

At 1:45, they hit the upper side of #1, and it got dark inside the woods almost immediately. It felt like it was almost 5 pm at night with these skies, and inside these tall trees, it may have been midnight!

Everyone's minds were on the mountain lion, no doubt, but they could not lift their heads off the trail. Even though they were headed down hill, there was one section they had to go up, and then make a steep left on a very narrow trail. One by one, with their left foot down, they started to maneuver the turn. The lightening was super bright, and the thunder was deafening.

They had to lean their bikes to the left, but not too far as to slide the rear end down the trail. The boys watched how Gage did it, but then, he made everything look so easy!

Bobby made it around, and you could tell how proud he was! "Great job Bobby," exclaimed DJ over the bike noise. DJ looked around for the deadly cat, but it appeared they had finally gotten rid of it.

It was Travis's turn, and as he started around the corner, a super loud thunder came rattling thru the forest, with a very loud noise to the left. Everyone looked, and this time, down went Travis!

He high-sided, throwing him down the hill inside the forest! Logan had jumped off his bike to make sure he could catch them, or their bikes…or both, if they had a misstep.

Travis had fallen down the hill about 15 feet, end over end…deep in bushes at the bottom! And he was scared to death!! DJ knew what to do, and he threw the rope back to Logan.

By now everyone had their bikes turned off. "I saw something in the woods," screamed Travis. "It was like another person or something," said Travis, now almost crying hysterically. "Hey we got you," said Logan. "Tie the rope around your waist," as Logan threw the rope down to him.

"Dig your heels in, and hang onto the rope," yelled DJ down to him. He was amazed how far he gone down the hill, or how he even went down there at all…it was steep! It took about 5 minutes for Logan and DJ to pull him up, a minute at a time.

Thank God his bike stayed up on the trail!

You could see how DJ was getting a little frustrated, not at the boys, but at the situation, and probably thinking they should not have done this to begin.

Maybe this was not a good idea!

By the time Travis reached the top, DJ had him take his helmet off, clean himself off, which, with the rain still coming down, it was not hard to get clean. "Hey I am telling you I saw something", said Travis. "I saw it right over there," pointing slightly to the left of where he was standing by his bike. Travis was still exhausted.

He kept yelling about what he saw, "Hey Travis, okay, let's relax we still have a big stream to get across," said Logan. "I saw it too"!

Everyone looked at Logan, because if another of the boys saw it…and it was LOGAN that saw it, then there had to be something out there. "Holy crap, let's get out of here," said Charlie in a scared voice.

"BRAOOOOROOORAAAR" came this weird howling noise, and it was not like wolves. "What the HELL is that," asked Bobby. The boys were now super quiet for a few seconds. "Oh my god," said Gage. "Let's get OUT of here"!

DJ said to all of them as they got on their bikes, "EYES ON THE TRAIL," exclaimed DJ. "DO NOT LOOK UP," we are going to be just fine"!! But it was obvious DJ was worried too, because he made sure his Glock was fully loaded.

"Travis, you good to go," asked Gage? "Yes, let's get out of here"! It was a very good thing the boys had trained and gotten a lot stronger.

"The noise was now behind and to the left side!

"BRAOOOOROOORAAAR" ….This howling was clearly was not like any wolves or noise they had ever heard before!!

The bikes started up, and one by one they started pulling out of there, with DJ leading the way. The boys were going slow, with the trail being so wet and slippery. But they were riding well, considering the crappy conditions of the trails.

It was now close to 3 pm, rain slowing just slightly, thunder and lightning pounding, cracking and lighting up the forest! About 1o minutes after Travis's fall, they reached the stream they had to cross.

The water was easily running twice as strong as it was when they were on the way up.

"Holy crap that water is moving so fast," exclaimed DJ! Gage pulled ahead of DJ, he already had it planned how he was going to get across…there was only one way…GUN IT!!

Before he went across, DJ had him hold up. "I want us to get the other boys across," said DJ. "But I don't see how they can get across without sliding down the water…and that would be a disaster"! By now Logan had walked up to DJ and Gage. "I don't see a way across other than riding…they can do it," said Logan, looking back at the other boys.

"Hey guys if we were back home riding, you wouldn't hesitate to get across, so just be confident, and keep your weight BACK," said Logan in a very strong tone. He knew they had to get across here, and then the rest should be okay.

Key word is should be okay…they all knew they would never forget this ride the rest of their lives!

Gage started his bike up, he gunned the motor, and he hit the stream with his weight as far back as he could get it. Once he hit the middle of the stream, making his front wheel as light as he could! His bike bogged down a little, which showed Logan that they needed more speed by the time they hit the stream.

"Okay, back up, guys," let me go next, we need more speed," said Logan. And without hesitation, he hit the stream full speed in first gear. A massive splash of water came up, and he made it across no problem! Both Gage and Logan got off their bikes to help if needed. "Let's go, Bobby…don't hesitate…full speed first gear," yelled Gage back to him. The water was loud!

Bobby hit the water, he made it across with zero problems. Bobby's confidence was growing by the hour on this ride! "C'mon boys you got this," said DJ under his breath to himself. The rain was really starting to come down hard, and it seemed like in the last 10 minutes, it had gotten MUCH stronger…and we still had Charlie, Travis and DJ to get across.

As Charlie lined up to take his turn, he hesitated, and DJ saw it. Ofcourse these boys were hesitating at THIS point…the water was definitely faster!

"Wait," yelled DJ. He was standing behind Charlie, and Charlie could barely hear him, but Gage saw DJ waving his arms, and Gage waved at the boys to stop for a hot minute.

DJ walked to his left to look for a way to get the boys across the water, so that Gage or Logan could get the bikes across. It was getting scary!

One of the reasons the water was moving so dang fast at this point was because two streams came together. DJ found a place just upstream that just might work to get them across one stream at a time. They had to jump across a rock in each place, then they finish to get to the other side by walking down a slippery hill. This was much safer.

"Gage, Logan, walk up that hill, cross over on that rock, and ride their bikes across," yelled DJ. "Charlie, Travis, you come up here where I am…and go down the opposite way, and let's move FAST"!

It was still a scary deal, with the water getting faster by the minute, even in the single stream. The boys on both sides of what was now almost a river, moved as fast as they could!

Gage and Logan jumped across first, showing Travis and Charlie the way. All of the boys made it across with no issues. The thunder was deafening, and the lightening made it look like daylight.

The boys got ready to walk down the hill, and to the left, Travis sees 150 feet in front of him the same thing he saw when he fell! "DJ," yelled Travis…LOOOK"!! "Charlie you see what I see," questioned Travis.

DJ jumped across as fast as he could. It was amazing how strong and quick DJ was, and he was there in just 10 seconds. "What did you see Travis," questioned DJ. "Look, it is right behind that tree," said Travis, pointing to the tree 100-150 feet in front of them. But it was dark in there again, even with their flashlights guiding the way.

Whatever it was, they couldn't see it now. DJ held his light on the tree, moving from side to side to try and get a different angle, but nothing was there.

"Okay, guys, I believe you, but right now let's get down the hill carefully, and get ready to get the hell out of here," said DJ. The rain was steady, and for the last minute or so, no thunder and lightning. But the rain kept coming!

Gage and Logan each grabbed a bike. They treated it like a Supercross start…grabbing the front brake, getting weight forward, turned up the throttle, and dumped the clutch! As Gage got ready to hit the water, he moved his weight way back, and kept the throttle turned wide open!

DJ couldn't believe just how good these two boys were at riding, and how poised they were. Gage made everything look extremely simple. Next was Logan, and as he was getting across the far side, his wheel hit the edge, and it jack-knived him over. Travis and Charlie ran over to help him up, and he popped right up.

"DJ, you should have Gage ride your bike across," yelled Logan. "This thing is a bitch"! DJ jumped off his bike, and by that time, Gage had already started back over to get DJ's bike across. The water continued to rise, which made jumping across the two streams even harder.

By the time DJ made it to the other side, Gage had gunned the bike and flown across the water. There was no screwing around, time to get moving! "Sheriff do you hear me," asked DJ across his radio. "We are probably 30-45 min away from hitting Eagle Crossing."

"Hey, DJ, I hear you," said the Sheriff. "We had to get a dozer to get the water off the road, and it just got started. I'm thinking we can get there about the time you get there. And we're bringing the fire department, to help get across the river, which is moving superfast"!

DJ gave the news to the boys, and they started to move out!

That stream that turned into a fast river debacle took almost a full hour of time. Now 4:15 pm, it was getting darker and darker. The lightening was good for helping to guide the way. Hopefully, it would be smooth sailing to EC! One steep trail to get down, DJ stopped at the top. Gage knew to move ahead and show them the way down.

"Stand up, get your weight slightly back, stay almost off the front brake entirely," yelled Gage back to everyone else. And down he went, slowly, smoothly, until he got to flat ground. As Gage looked back, he heard this super loud grunt to his right. CRAP, a HUGE moose was there, not even 50 feet away. A scared, mean moose can be dangerous!! "DJ, hurry," yelled Gage. As DJ got to the bottom, Gage had moved behind his bike, but if the moose charged, that bike wouldn't help! "Iam guessing that, like the mountain lion, this is a mother moose," said DJ in a loud voice, hoping it would scare the moose away.

"Wait boys," yelled DJ back to the boys up the hill. "My god can anything else happen tonight" questioned DJ as he shook his head. The rain was getting even stronger. DJ pulled out his pistol, and waived it around trying to decide where he would fire his warning shot. He slowly squeezed the trigger above the moose, and BAMM, it startled the moose. He moved away just a tiny bit, which told DJ that she was guarding her young baby.

"Okay, let's go," yelled DJ. He kept his eye on the moose, and one by one, down they came without any problems. And once again, off they went, the time was now 4:45.

DJ was hoping they would hit EC at 4 pm or earlier, but everything that could happen…happened! He could tell they were about 10 to 15 minutes from the front edge of #1, and the rest of the trail should be smooth.

FINALLY, they reached the front edge of #1, and from here, they had about 1.5 miles away to reach EC. DJ raised his hand to get the boys to stop before they got out of forest. He knew there were small groups of trees to hide in when they got there. He knew getting across was going to take the fire department's help.

"Okay, ride quick but smooth, when we get to EC, we hide under the trees," said DJ. "We are going to leave the bikes at the river"! The boys hadn't thought about that yet, but they certainly knew it made sense.

"I am sooo damn proud of you boys," exclaimed DJ, as he went to each guy high fiving them. They looked down at the river, realizing just how fast that water was moving. "DJ, how in the world are we getting across THAT water," asked Charlie. "Not to mention…. up the hill"??

"The firemen got this," said DJ. "If we can get down the mountain and get this far…hey, the rest can't be too hard"! Charlie leaned on his seat, and prayed. "Dear God…guide the firemen in getting us across safely"! The boys had all gotten a look at the water, and had NO idea how they were going to get across.

Finally, the boys could see the high beams from the Sheriff and the fire truck coming thru with flashing lights. "YES…FINALLY," said all the boys at the same time! Finally, into view came the Sheriff's truck and the Fire Captain's truck, both 4-wheel drive. They for sure would not have been able to get a fire truck back here!

But how were they going to get across the water?

The rain slowed, and the thunder & lightening also slowed a little. "Hey, Charlie…great prayer, dude," said DJ with a smile. "Boys, keep your helmets and gloves on for now"! They all walked toward the ledge to look at the water, trying to wonder how in the world they would get over there.

"Hey, DJ, we aren't gonna have to spend the night over here, are we," asked Travis. He had a way of letting his mind get ahead of himself, and that is when panic sets in for Travis.

"No way in hell, Travis," said DJ. I am sure they have a plan"!

"Okay DJ, the fireman are coming down, get the boys to the bottom on your side," said the Sheriff. DJ looked back at the boys, looking to make sure everyone was ready with backpacks, gloves and helmets.

"No way anyone is getting over here to the bikes, but let's get them close together, and put your keys in your backpacks," said DJ. The boys all lined them up together, with Travis and Bobby's bikes on the outside, their kickstands were not great.

"Bobby and I can't get our keys out," said Travis. "Don't sweat it," said Logan. "Let's get down the hill." Logan was all business, always getting to the point.

They looked across EC, and saw 3 firemen getting ready to go down the other hill. You could tell they were busy organizing a plan to get them across. The water looked even faster than 10 minutes ago. It was now 6 pm, and everyone was absolutely exhausted!!

There was no walking down the hill, it was too wet and too slippery. So, they kneeled down and slid down on their heels. By the time they reached the bottom, DJ could see the plan unfolding…it involved a raft, lots of ropes and life vests.

One by one they used ropes to get the raft from one side to the other. The boys put on the vest, got in the raft, and they pulled the raft over to the side. Finally, something that was going right!

"Okay boys, I'm Captain Stone, we are going to use a long strap tied around your waist, pulling up 3 at a time. Let's double-time it, boys, we need to get out of this lightening!

And just like that, they were up at the top, dehydrated, super hungry, and very tired.

Chloe jumped out of the Sheriff's truck, and came over to give Logan a big hug. Logan was a little embarrassed, not to mention a little shy. But they talked for a second, no doubt Logan was telling her about their day.

"Boys, after you get cleaned up, are you too tired to eat at the diner"? They all looked at each other, Gage said "are you kidding, I'm in…I am sooo hungry"!

"Sheriff, have you ever heard of these guys who live on the mountain, or IN the mountain," asked DJ. "Yeah, well, I heard stories about this…they called them the 'Forest Dwellers'," said the Sheriff. "But had no idea if it was real."

"Well, the Dwellers are for real," said DJ very emphatically. "We'll talk about it at dinner."

"See you boys in 45 min, get cleaned up, can't wait to hear about this trip," said the Sheriff. "You firemen, you're coming too"!

When the Sheriff talks, people listen!

CHAPTER 7

Nobody Saw This Coming

It was fantastic having everyone back safe and sound, and having dinner at the diner with parents, the Sheriff, firemen, and seeing everyone thanking DJ for leading everyone back obviously made DJ feel like a million bucks. And dinner was paid by the Sheriff's office, including all the boy's families.

"I want to thank everyone for being here," said Sheriff Weldon. "I've also invited the folks from Whispering Pines who also were robbed. Well, we got some of their items back, thanks to these brave guys called the Moto Boys, led by our incredible Deputy John, we call him DJ"!

"Hey folks, you can identify your stolen items, and we will mark it down, "said Deputy Colton. "We have to hang onto these items for now, and it's too bad we couldn't get it all back. Hopefully soon."

With that, DJ and Deputy Colton put the recovered items on a neighboring table. By then, other people in the diner had caught on to what was going on, and they came back, applauding when the folks were handed back what was mostly jewelry.

The Sheriff noticed one couple sitting in a booth, acting like they were completely ignoring what was going on. Strange…when everyone else that within earshot of the group, was standing, participating, smiling, and genuinely happy with this celebration.

"Hey, Sheriff, do we get to go to Silver Mines again?" Bobby began, but the Sheriff subtly waved him off, his eyes never leaving the booth. As soon as he made the motion, the couple stirred, shifting in their seats for the first time.

The Sheriff didn't trust these people. He wasn't exactly sure why yet; it was just instinct.

"Okay, guys, let's finish up, and I want to see you guys at the office tomorrow night," said the Sheriff. "Again, I want to thank you boys for everything," as everyone clapped and cheered for them. For everything they went through, what an amazing feeling it must have been!

The boys couldn't wait to have their meeting with the Sheriff on Monday night; they were certain that they were going to lay out their plans to hit the offenders in the mansions, which the boys also called them "The Haunted Mansions." Dinner for the Dalton brothers went quickly, even though they had invited Chloe and Emma over for dinner.

Margie wanted to give her two cents about "not wanting the boys to go on the next trip," as she had heard the night before about the dangers of getting to Silver Mines. But, she didn't say anything with the girls there, for fear of the boys getting embarrassed.

"Okay, Dad, let's go! You guys ready to go too," asked Logan looking at the girls. "Oh, we get to go too," asked Chloe. They all piled into Jacob Dalton's truck. "I have a plan for the mansions, said Logan, with Gage's eyes getting wide. "Logan, tell me," said Gage. Logan just waved his hand, as to say "not now."

"What are the mansions?" said Emma. At 14, she was often included, though not always tuned. But the boys were always respectful and nice to her, particularly since Logan liked her sister.

"The mansions are these massive, beautiful homes just outside of the ghost town of Silver Mines," said Logan. "It's this one street of mansions that is actually called The Silver Mines Estates." Logan, being patient, waited to make sure Emma understood.

"Silver Mines used to be a rich town because of mining gold and silver. And people used their money to build these beautiful homes with huge oak trees along the streets, said Logan. "In Silver Mines, they mined both silver and gold, so at one time there was a LOT of money."

"But…the super creepy thing about 'The Estates' is that it's supposedly haunted," said Logan. Both of the girls shivered, Emma said, "for real…are you being serious"?

"Yeah, I read a story that the mansions definitely are filled with ghosts," said Gage. "I can't wait to get in there"! No way to really tell if Gage was excited to go inside one of the mansions.

"Hey, Logan, how scary can it be if those idiots are going in the houses?" Gage asked. Logan just shrugged; he was focused on the meeting ahead.

Chloe had heard the story before about these haunted houses, but Emma looked genuinely spooked. She knew about Silver Mines – but, was clueless about the haunting mansions.

All the boys arrived at the station together, with their dads walking in behind them. The Sheriff welcomed them all in, and he was pretty jovial. DJ and Deputy Colton, however, were all business – stone-faced at the front of the room. Logan, who was very perceptive, picked up on this and walked up to DJ.

"What's happening?" Logan said. DJ just whispered, "Not now; we'll talk in a minute."

"Okay, guys, grab a seat, we have a ton of info to share. I want to remind all of you, that you are deputized as Cadets, so this information does not get outside of these walls. And this goes for both the girls and your parents"! They all nodded, YES quickly, with no one uttering a single word.

"First, this is much bigger than we first thought, with robberies now extending into other parts of Montana, and over four new one's last week alone in Billings, Kalispell, and Columbia," exclaimed the Sheriff. "And several new ones in Boise that resembled the same type of robberies"!

Sheriff quietly observed the room's atmosphere briefly. "We have a mess on our hands," said the Sheriff. "It's clear that this group is feeling pretty damn brave, and obviously has an inside track as to when people are going to be out of their homes," said Deputy Colton.

"And evidently, they're using these areas like Silver Mines and the mansions, I guess you guys call it The Estates or the Mansions, as their distribution points," said the Sheriff.

You could tell the Sheriff was struggling slightly with this new nomenclature. After all, there was "EC, OG, #1, #2," but "Silver Mines," was always called "Silver Mines."

The boys all looked at each other as if to say "we can't believe we get to be a part of this"! No question this was so different than the first time the Dalton's were robbed!

"Like the Sheriff said last night, we couldn't be prouder of the job you guys did," said DJ. "I know I in particular couldn't be prouder of you boys, from recovering from falls down the mountains, to getting away from the criminals, a mountain lion...even a DAMN moose," exclaimed DJ!

"But," said DJ, with his tone changing fast, "this is too dangerous for you guys. It was dangerous for ME," said DJ. "You can't blame this on the Sheriff, this was me telling the Sheriff it was too dangerous, and we can't put you in harm's way again, even if we have trouble catching them"!

The room was silent. Logan could feel this coming on when he saw DJ's expression when they walked in. No one knew what to say, except Logan. "Okay, Sheriff, Deputy Colton, and DJ," said Logan, what if I had a way that was both safe, and exposed this operation in the Mansions"! By now, Logan was standing up, wanting to move to the marker board to show the plan. He was NOT going to hear a no!

"Wait, guys," said Travis, interrupting. "I can back out, to make it easier for you guys, if you want"! Logan didn't hesitate. He didn't want to make it look like that would change his plan at all.

"Hey, I have a plan for you, Travis, you'll see," said Logan. By now, all of the boys were sitting on the edge of the seats. But the only opinions that mattered were at the front of the room.

"Well, hey, we owe you boys at least that much," said Sheriff. Logan had only shared this plan with his dad right before dinner. Logan looked up at his dad for a second, and Jacob gave him a quick nod with a wink of approval.

"Let's hear it," said DJ. You could tell that DJ was really hoping it was solid.

Logan drew a map from Eagle Crossing, including #1, #2, the Silver Mines Ghost Town, and even the stores in the ghost town, all the way up to the Mansions. Logan also made a "legend" on the map for the abbreviations they were using. He did this for the parents in the room, plus the Sheriff.

EC: Eagle Crossing

#1: Forest #1

#2: Forest #2 SM: Silver Mines

WS: Whispering Pines CS: Clear Springs

"First, this is going to be safe on three fronts," said Logan, who was sounding very assuring. "Number one, the weather looks safe over the next week. Two, you guys come from the other direction. Three, all we do is locate where they are at, we never come in contact with them, and you guys come up the road and nail them!

DJ, Sheriff, and Deputy Colton (DC) started firing off questions on the details, and Logan had all the answers, or at least most of the answers. They covered more details for another 15 minutes.

Finally, Jacob spoke up. "Hey Sheriff, everything …and I mean everything, went wrong on this trip for these boys, yet none of them got hurt, and they were ready for dinner at the Diner that night," reminded Jacob.

"If we do nothing, not only do they get away with the robberies, but the people in Clear Springs and Whispering Pines are not safe right now, so we have to get a step ahead of them"!

DJ clearly wanted another mission with the boys, not to mention a chance to get these idiots, and was definitely in favor of this plan. "Hey Sheriff, we can make this work," said DJ. "This is much safer than mission #1"!

The Sheriff peeled off to have a quiet chat with Deputy Colton and DJ. Logan couldn't make out what they were saying, but clearly, the Sheriff was talking the most. Finally, they broke out of their huddle, and Sheriff went to the podium.

"Okay, we can live with this plan," said Sheriff. "You parents have the final say. Are you all in favor of this plan, too?" asked the Sheriff.

"You will have to sign off on this mission, AND, I'll say this…if any of you, or the boys, are not comfortable with this trip, just say the word, we are just as proud of you"!

The boys all looked at each other in an approving nod. "I want back in," said Travis! Logan felt bad for Travis, but he had already carved out a plan for him to help, so he would be included, just not on the bike.

"Hey Travis, I think we stick with the new plan, that way you can help on the other end of this trip," said Logan. Travis nodded yes with a smile.

Deep down even Travis was glad he was not going back thru the forests and eventually riding into the mansions! That was how Logan was…he knew how to make everyone feel better about themselves!

"Okay, tomorrow we have to try and get the bikes back," said DJ. "The water should be down enough, let's meet at 4 pm after you get out of school at the entrance to EC"!

The boys had homework, and were still exhausted, so off they went in their own directions, until tomorrow.

Early October in Clear Springs was cool and breezy, particularly in late afternoon. The skies were clear, with no rain on the horizon. DJ, Bobby's dad, and Jacob all drove their trucks in to get the boys bikes. The road was still muddy, but four-wheel drive made it easy to get to Eagles Crossing.

"Okay, guys, let's get across," said DJ, after everyone had their bikes off the trucks. "This is not going to be fun because of the mud climb, but I have some water, so we can get our hands clean before riding out." From where they were, they couldn't see their bikes, but they knew where to go!

The water was still moving pretty fast, and it was not going to be a piece of cake getting across. Once they got to the bottom of the ravine of Eagle Crossing, the boys had to back-track to a place where there were rocks they could walk across. They still had to get the bikes across.

"Guys, this thing is a piece of cake to get across," said Gage, being Gage. That gave the boys some confidence. Then again…it was Gage saying it. They started up the hill, realizing now they should have started earlier…already getting dark fast!!

They climbed to the top, quickly cleaned their hands, and headed over to the bikes. As they got close, they realized something looked wrong— really wrong!

"What the hell?" said DJ! They were missing Travis's and Bobby's bikes!!

As Bobby and Travis walked up to bikes, and seeing their bikes missing, both of them almost started crying. "Are you kidding me? You have to be kidding me," said Bobby!!

"What in the world happened?" DJ asked to himself! "Hey Sheriff come in," said DJ. "I'm here, what's up?" said Sheriff. DJ walked away from the boys, even though the boys knew exactly what he was saying.

"You are not going to believe this, but Travis's and Bobby's bikes are missing," said DJ. "We looked around a little bit, but no sign of them so far."

Nothing came back from the Sheriff, at first. "Sheriff you there?" asked DJ.

"Yeah I'm here, first of all, put Travis and Bobby on can you," asked the Sheriff. As DJ put his phone on speaker, "Hey boys, I want you to know that if we don't find your bikes in perfect condition, and I mean perfect condition, the Sheriff department is buying you guys brand new bikes, and I mean, it happens right away"!

Travis and Bobby looked at each other with a smile on their faces, as if to say, "hopefully they don't find the bikes." Both Travis and Bobby's bikes were a little older, and needed a fair amount of work to keep up with the other boys' bikes.

"Hey, DJ," said the Sheriff, "we have an active investigation happening tonight, so back to HQ when done, please." With Deputy Colton getting older, and not as active as in years past, Sheriff Weldon had become very reliant on DJ, and DJ could feel the love certainly coming back his way!

"Okay see you soon Sheriff," said DJ. Right now, we gotta get out of here, it is getting dark," said DJ. "Let's stop looking for now, let's move out…NOW." The boys fired up the bikes, and they decided that Travis would ride with Logan, and Bobby would ride up with Gage. "Hey guys, the three of us will come back here and go looking for the bikes," said DJ, talking to Gage and Logan.

"Okay, we should start riding at 3 pm tomorrow from this side," said Logan. "Somehow I don't think we're gonna find them, but hey, we gotta try," said Gage. "Hop on, guys, let's go…hang on tight"!

Gage went first, and even with Bobby riding with him, Gage stood up to ride down the hill. When he made it down, Bobby hopped off to walk up the trail, cross the rocks, and then back to where Gage & Logan were waiting. Travis and Bobby crossed the stream together…carefully!

By now, word had gotten back to Bobby & Travis's families about the missing bikes; it was definitely a welcome message that the department would pick up the cost of new bikes, IF they couldn't find them! Neither family had the money for used bikes, let alone new bikes! The boys would sleep good tonight!

DJ was starving, so they met in the back booth at the diner. "DJ, we have some intel, you remember that couple I was talking about last night," asked Sheriff. DJ motioned yes, and kept powering down his roast beef dinner. "Get this, said Deputy Colton, "we believe they're feeding those guys information about families that could be worth robbing."

DJ kept eating, shaking his head back and forth, trying to understand the whole situation. "How did you find out they are involved," asked DJ. "Well, said the Sheriff, Logan and Gage's mom was here the other day, sitting in a booth in back of them. She had zero idea who they were sitting next to, but…she started hearing reference to Bob, Larry, and even Max"!

"And no way that is a coincidence," said Deputy Colton. "We just heard about this on Saturday when you guys were up in the mountains," said Sheriff. "So, we're gonna pay them a visit tomorrow night, we're trying to get a warrant to check their house"!

"For now, only the three of us know about this," said Sheriff. DJ had eaten his dinner, and motioned for dessert. The Sheriff and Deputy Colton were always amazed how much DJ could eat and be in perfect shape.

"Okay, Gage, Logan and I are going to at least look around to see if we can find the bikes," said DJ. "I don't have my hopes up, and have zero idea who could have taken them. I don't see how it could be Bob's gang, and there is no one in this town that knows how to get over Eagle Crossing"!

Next day, Gage, Logan, and DJ met with small backpacks at Eagle's Crossing. They fired up the bikes and headed over the ravine, keeping an eye out for the bikes along the trail up to #1. It was now 2:30, the weather this whole week had been clear, and getting cooler by the day. After all this was Montana in the beginning of Fall.

Gage led the way up to the start of #1, with DJ taking the lead into the forest. The three of them kept a fast pace for about 10 minutes, when Gage slowed the pace so they could start looking around. Both Gage and Logan had new 6,000-lumen portable spotlights strapped to their sleeves, and DJ had a 20,000-lumen spotlight, with another set of lights on the handlebars.

They stopped, turned their bikes off, and once again, the eerie, creepy sounds of the deep forest came out loud and clear. They could hear wolves howling in the distance, the wind whirring thru the trees. You could hear animals breaking through small branches, but no sight of any dangerous creatures, at least yet.

It was crazy how things looked with these lights, "Okay, let's keep moving, said DJ. "BRAOOOOROOORAAAR" came the creepiest noise, like before, only MUCH louder!! "What the hell is THAT," asked Logan. All three of them started crouching down, looking around in every direction. It was the scariest sound they have ever heard…even for DJ!

"It sounds like some kind of howling monkey…or something," said Gage. "Holy Crap"!!!

"Should we get the hell out of here DJ," asked Gage. "Naw, let's keep going just a little bit, let's get past the water, and make a decision from there," said DJ. "But no question this is even freaking me out too!!

The sound continued as they started on the trail, DJ keeping all his light power on, he could on the surroundings.

They came up to an opening in the woods, probably 5 minutes away from the water. It was a good place to look around, and they decided to get off the bikes and walk a little bit, which seemed like a bad idea to Logan. "Hey, DJ, I just think we stay close to the bikes, yes," asked Logan.

A sound up the trail and to the right made DJ kept walking up the trail, now a little faster. He pulled out his P320, and by now, all 3 of them were super quiet! Logan and Gage caught up to DJ, Gage and Logan were trying to be quiet on their breathing.

Out of the corner of DJ's eye, he saw some low branches move, the bush was dark deep green with the light on it. And standing directly above, 150 feet in front of them, was the thing that Travis said he saw, and that Logan thought he saw!!

Now, the 3 of them start gazing at one another, but two slightly aborigine-looking men…at least they looked like they were aborigine, or indigenous?! The boys and DJ kept their lights fixed on them. They stood perfectly still, with what appeared to be a bow and arrow, the one on the right was holding.

The closer they got to them, the more normal they looked, except, it looked like they had a small bone in their right ear lobe. They wore a bearskin overcoat with a bear head, no doubt to keep them warm in the winter months. No doubt this was the strangest, scariest scene imaginable!!

"Holy shit DJ, what the hell do we do here," said Gage. The boys were scared. DJ was scared!!

Suddenly, the noise was coming from behind the 3 of them… "BRAOOOOROOORAAAR." They whirled around to see what was in back of them, which was nothing! They swirled back where their first position, and now they were not there.

"BRAOOOOROOORAAAR" came from up the trail, and now in back of them. BAAAM, BAAAM fired DJ, not at them, but slightly above them. It scared the crap of the boys. The noise stopped, and they moved off the trail. DJ shined his light at them again, but this time the noise they made was absolutely deafening…. "BRAOOOOROOORAAAR"…. "BRAOOOOROOORAAAR."

DJ considered firing directly at them, but thought better of it. "Okay, the search is over, let's get out of here…I couldn't care less about the bikes," said DJ. They fired up the bikes, took one look around, and were made record time down the trail. About 5 minutes from the bottom side of #1, right off the trail was Travis's bike, which was severely wrecked.

The front wheel was completely ruined, the seat was torn up, and the gas tank looked as if it was almost ripped off! Logan pulled out his phone to take some pics, while DJ held the light on the bike. Gage kept his lights on the bushes on both sides. Clearly, this was the absolute scariest and eery night of their lives!

"Hey guys, DJ whispered, these guys have no Interest in hurting us, is my guess, otherwise they would have shot an arrow at us." But, they aren't going to let us hurt them either."

"What does this bike message mean, DJ?" asked Logan. "Hey, you're the smart guy, you tell me," said DJ to Logan. "Let's get out of here, this is a night we'll never forget," said Gage!

CHAPTER 8

On That Trail Again

One thing you can always count on is DJ being hungry. Deputy Colton, Sheriff and DJ met at the diner in their back booth, like they always do, away from people in the front.

Most of the time people left them alone, and every now and then someone just had to come up and say hi. Sheriff was pretty good at saying hi and at the same time letting them know, "hey we can't talk right now!"

"Okay I am telling you that trip into #1 was unbelievable, scary, creepy…you name it," said DJ. There, standing right in front of us, in the super dark woods, was these aborigine looking people, bone in the upper lip, holding an arrow, bear skin over their bodies to keep them warm, with a sound like a howler monkey," exclaimed DJ. "They could have hurt us, and…I could have shot them too, so I think as long as we leave each other alone…we'll be fine," said DJ a little quieter this time.

"Logan showed us what howler monkeys sound like, and sure enough it did, just a little deeper and creepier sounding," said DJ.

"What about the bike thing," asked Deputy Colton. "That makes zero sense, they can't ride the bikes"! DJ just shook his head, "I have no idea," but, Sheriff, do you want me to look for new bikes for Travis and

Bobby," asked DJ.

"Yes, let's move on those bikes immediately," said the Sheriff. "That is the least we can do for Bobby and Travis."

"Listen, right now we don't have enough information to get a warrant," said the Sheriff. "But, the Sheriff of Kalispell said they just had 6 new robberies, four were businesses, and two were home robberies"! Sheriff realized he was talking too loudly, so lowering his voice, "they used to average one robbery maybe every other month…now six in a week," exclaimed the Sheriff!

Deputy Colton lowered his head, brought his voice way down… "and guess who always seems to come to the diner when we are here…this," as he nodded his head a couple of booths away from them! "The diner has cameras, and the night that Bob and Larry characters came and created that chaos, guess who was here"!

"So…we did a drive by earlier today," said Sheriff. "We ran the plates on their other car, and it's in the husband's name, and guess what, he is related to Bob, his name is Leo"!

DJ couldn't believe what he was hearing. "So somehow they're feeding intel to these three," asked DJ. He was smart…very smart, and was trying to piece this together. "No doubt we are way behind on what is going on, they could be the brains behind this, or, maybe they are being forced to give them information," said DJ.

"Okay, DJ, for now, are we set on the plan for Eagles Crossing, or as you call it, EC," asked the Sheriff. "Yep, and we are going over it one last time tomorrow, making sure Charlie knows his role, and that everyone is safe," said DJ.

"I am looking forward to rolling out Friday morning, Travis and Bobby are riding with you in the truck, right," asked DJ. Sheriff nodded his head yes, getting up out of the booth, and walked directly over to the booth to the mystery couple.

"Hey folks, I haven't had the pleasure of meeting you, I'm Sheriff Weldon, this is Deputy Colton, and Deputy JJ," said the Sheriff, shaking their hands. "Oh, nice to meet you Sheriff…and Deputies, I'm Leo and this is Karen," said Leo. They all shook hands, Karen glancing up very quickly but then looking down away from the three of them.

"Leo remained smiling, acting very cool. He tried to keep the conversation light. "It is getting nippy out there, isn't it," said Leo in kind of a laughing tone. The Sheriff really wanted to ask Leo and Karen questions, but right now was not the right time.

"It sure is getting nippy," said Deputy Colton. "Well, nice to meet you folks, have a great night," said DJ. And out they walked. Once they got outside, they continued until they were out of sight. DJ glanced back inside without them seeing him, and he could see that they were arguing about something. "Well, they are nervous about something," said DJ.

"Hey, Sheriff, can I go sit on their house and see if I can listen in," asked DJ. "I think you get your sleep, let's not take any chances, because it is not going to change our plan on Friday," said Sheriff.

"Let's get some sleep"!

Friday morning was here, and the boys were loaded up, in the truck and headed over to Eagle Crossing. Chloe was of course, riding over in the truck to see the boys off. "Hope we don't have trouble with the Howlers," said Logan, so that only Chloe could hear. "Stop it Logan," exclaimed Chloe. "I'm scared enough"! Logan smiled and said "Hey

I'm just kidding, it will be fine," said Logan. He gave her a hug, as well as his mom and dad. "See you all tonight," said Gage.

DJ looked out over the boys, looking for them to give the thumbs up. They fired up the bikes, and Gage led them off. All the parents, and Chloe, watched them as they easily got down and then up the other side. All the boys stopped at the top, and waved back at the parents. Chloe and Logan had a secret two-handed wave with each other.

The boys' mom came up and gave Chloe a hug, seeing that she had tears going down her cheeks. "Sweetie they will be juuuust fine," said Margie. "You going to ride with the Sheriff tonight?" asked Jacob, the boys' dad. "I would not miss it for the world," said Chloe.

The boys hit lower side of #1 in record time, the weather was clear, and the dirt was perfect for riding. DJ, taking his turn at the front, was clearly the third best rider now out of the group. Charlie was now fourth best, and was gaining confidence every time he went out riding.

They got to the stream inside #1, and without any trouble or needing to change riders, they all made it across. Both Gage and Logan were carrying extra gas for the group in a small pack strapped to the back of their seats, just in case they needed it. They were moving with great precision on this ride.

And no sign of the Howlers! What they didn't know is if the Howlers were also part of Forest #2, nor did they know how many Howlers. It would certainly make sense..the two forests were not far apart.

It was now 9:20 am as they got to the upper side of #1; they stopped for a sec, got a drink of water and a piece of jerky. "Hey DJ, I wonder if the grizzlies and the mountain lions can smell the jerky," asked Logan. "Actually, very good question I should have thought about that ahead of time," said DJ. "Let's eat quick, so we don't become lunch ourselves," said Charlie!

They saw a moose and a bull elk at the left edge of the meadow, and so far, no mountain lion. They had bear spray that they would use on any aggressive animal if needed!

"Sheriff, come in," radioed DJ. The last time they tried the Sheriff from this point, they could not get thru, but the weather was horrible. "Hey DJ, I can hear you, but not well," said Sheriff.

"We're making good time up the roads with Sheriff Joe from Kalispell. We're towing up a total of three Can-Am's" Both Sheriff departments knew people they could borrow Can-Am's from, they didn't have either the money in their budgets nor the time to go purchase Can-Am's for this trip.

"Tell Logan we got his plan lined up when we hit Silver Mines," said DC. It was going to require quick work by both Sheriffs, Deputy Colton and Dalton, who brought plenty of wood, saws, and other construction equipment.

This all had to happen once the sun set when they hit Silver Mines. They had to make basically get up to the bridge for the Estates, and hopefully over, without making too much noise.

On the boys' side of things, a lot of things had to go right for this plan to work:

1. Make Silver Mines *in record time*, get a quick rest, make sure none of the criminals are there, so they can continue to the mansions.

2. They had never been to the Mansions. Supposedly it wasn't far from the town of Silver Mines. They were going off of old maps. There was a bridge once upon a time to get over the river. The river and the bridge separated these huge mansions from town.

3. They had to park their bikes near the bridge, and walk in to the street of these 7 or 8 mansions. It was actually Chloe, her mom and Margie, the boys' mom, that found drawings of these

4. mansions. The old drawings they'd found showed how beautiful these houses were, showed also the massive oak trees along the street.

5. Find the mansion where they're hiding out…IF they 're even there!

6. Lead the Sheriffs and the Deputies right to where they are hiding out.

Sounds simple enough! No one believed for a second it would be simple!

There was no way to get into Silver Mines from the other side, without making an emergency makeshift bridge. That's where Jacob (Logan and Gage's dad), came in… As a builder, he knew how to get this makeshift bridge done. He brought the lumber and tools to get it done!

Then once the Sheriffs and the deputies were able to get across this bridge, they could bring the Can-Am's into where Bob, Larry and Max were going to be, it should be an easy arrest!

Now 11 am, they fired up the bikes, and within two minutes, they hit the lower side of #2. Both of the forests were single track, but the thing about #2, it was a single track trail with overgrown bush on both sides, so they had to go a little slower than going thru #1. Number 2 forest was definitely steeper than number 1 forest.

They made it to the log, and one by one, they made it over, with Gage leading them over. He did it without even putting his foot down! Charlie had to have some help on this one, and Gage went ahead and went thru the stream for him as well, while Charlie hiked up and over the stream. The thing about Charlie, he was such a nice kid with zero ego, and he just made things easy!

"BRAOOOOROOORAAAR"   ….   "BRAOOOOROOORAAAR"

Well, if there was ever a question of the Howlers being inside #2, that answered that question! Logan looked over at Charlie, and he could tell he was scared out of his mind. They all were scared! DJ pulled out his P320, and was looking around to see if he could see the Howlers.

"BRAOOOOROOORAAAR" ….it was to the right of them, and with his super bright spotlight, DJ saw them! "Look," said DJ, pointing to the right and slightly in back of them. "It's okay, Charlie, let's get going…at least you can say you now saw a Howler," said Logan.

As they turned to get going, up in front of them was a Howler…and now two Howlers, standing directly on the trail. SHIT!! What do we do now?? Is DJ going to shoot them? Yell at them? Would we ride right through them?

DJ whispered to us as he walked by us, "keep your heads on a slow swivel boy, let's be calm and cool." The larger Howler was holding his bow, but not holding it up, as if he was going to shoot anyone. "Do you speak English," asked DJ. They two howlers looked at each other, but did not respond to DJ.

The boys, particularly DJ, could see their features. They had a small curved bone pierced in the middle of their nose, almost like a mustache. They were in super shape, probably from running thru the forest all day. They both wore bearskin covers, that came down almost like a long jacket. Both of the Howlers kept their mouth closed for the most part, but DJ could tell they both had teeth missing.

"What language do you speak," DJ asked again, pointing to his mouth. The Howlers still not speaking, pointed to the spotlight. DJ turned it on for them, pointed it out into the forest. At this point, DJ just wanted to get going, but he remained cool, calm and collective. "Would you like it," said DJ, holding it out as a gift.

The smaller Howler gently held his hand out, and DJ handed it to him. "Ahhh," said DJ, "wait one second." DJ walked over to his bike to grab another battery out of the pack on his back fender. Walking back over to the Howlers, "here is how you change a battery when it gets low or goes out." He had zero idea if they understood him when he showed them how to change out the battery.

DJ thought about trying to shake their hand, but thought better of it. He nodded to them and said "thank you for sharing your trail with us"!

"Now we have to go," motioning to them that they had to get moving. "The Howlers moved off the trail, and as the boys rode by, they did their traditional sound…no doubt hearing it up close was scary and still creepy.

"BRAOOOOROOORAAAR"   ...   "BRAOOOOOROOORAAAR"

…so clearly, they made this noise when they were apparently happy and felt threatened. Charlie did not look up as he rode by, both Gage and Logan, however, nodded and smiled at them as they rode by, Gage even said, "thank you."

They started riding a little faster to make up time. That whole thing took about 20-25 minutes! At the upper end of #2, they stopped for a quick drink and slammed a protein bar. "Holy crap DJ," exclaimed Gage. "A spotlight for passage on the trail"?

"Can you even believe what just happened," said DJ. "If I told my friends at school about this, they would say I'm crazy," said Charlie, Logan glanced out in the meadow to make sure nothing was going to jump out and get them, "hey guys, obviously we are going to tell our families…but let's not tell ANYONE at school," said Logan. "First of all, they would say we're crazy, second, they would want us to prove it.

"I snuck a couple of pics," said Gage. He handed his phone around to everyone, and sure enough, when DJ turned on the light, you could see them. They looked as if it were someone in the indigenous forests of the Amazon!

"I have never been more scared in my life," said Charlie! Gage looked around, out to the meadow, "look…three wolves over there," said Gage pointing to the left. "They aren't going to be a problem, we gotta get a move on, it's almost 3 pm," said DJ. "We have to get out of Silver Mines no later than 5 pm"

That's one of the things everyone loved about DJ, his understanding their schedule. "Now we can fly for the next ten minutes," said Gage, taking the lead for now. They got up to where they hid their bikes in 9 minutes, all of them had the throttles almost wide open. Gage's riding style was just so good, standing up most of the way, in full attack mode!

They all stopped where they were out of sight from anyone that could be looking down in Silver Mines. It was highly unlikely that any of the bad actors were even in Silver Mines, let alone be looking down. But DJ was not taking any chances.

"Okay, I am going to get up to Silver Mines, spend about ten minutes making sure no one is there, then we will just motor straight through. That is the plan at least," said DJ.

DJ triple-timed it up the hill, getting to the back side of Silver Mines. Now out of sight of the boys, he took a quick look down the street, and it was super quiet. Slightly breezy, with far off sounds of wolves howling. The boys decided not to pull any jerky out, in case it carried any scent to wolves or mountain lions. Jogging on the back side of Silver Mines, DJ got up to the backside of the saloon. Peeking around the corner where he last saw Bob, Larry and Max, he couldn't hear or see anything. He went to the front, and saw nothing inside the saloon.

The Silver Mines Ghost Town, in great shape considering. Once upon a time a robust and busy town. The School is behind this pic, with the Church straight ahead.

One quick trip over to the school where they had been hiding stolen goods, a few items were still there! Items like computers, some jewelry that DJ had not seen or recovered the last time. Now was not the time to get anything back, DJ ran as best he could down the hill and back to the boys.

"Okay, the coast is clear, let's get up the hill, I don't see any reason for us to stop in town," said DJ. "Yeah, it's getting dark, we're still behind schedule," said Logan.

The backside hill getting into Silver Mines was not small, and required the boys to hit it full throttle. Gage took off, and of course, he had no issues making it up the hill. Gage had taught all of them how to turn on a hill and get back down if they didn't make it.

Logan went next, and he made it no problem. Both Logan and Gage were in position to help if they did not make it up. Charlie went next. He was the lightest, but didn't have Gage's skill or speed. He hit the bottom with pretty good speed, but when he hit a huge bump about two-thirds up the hill, it bogged him down.

Charlie quickly laid the bike down like Gage had taught him, and remained calm. Gage had positioned himself down on the hill to help Charlie if needed. "Hey, Charlie, get on up to the top with Logan, I'll take a crack at it," said Gage.

"DJ go ahead, I'll go after you," said Gage. "Watch out for that huge bump in the middle of the hill." DJ positioned himself to go, but then motioned for Gage to go first. "I wanna watch how you hit that bump," said DJ. Gage took off, in a standing up, slightly crouched position, and as he hit the bump in the hill, he got over the handlebars, weight on the pegs, and like that, he shot over the top.

All Charlie could do is laugh, it was classic Gage riding style. DJ hit the throttle, and tried to emulate Gage and Logan's riding style as best he could. He got his front wheel to the top, barely, with Logan and Charlie pulling him over by grabbing his seat.

Finally, they were in Silver Mines, again, this time with their bikes!

CHAPTER 9

Adapt, Overcome and Improvise

S heriff come in, you there?" DJ said into his radio. "Yeah, we made it, DJ," said the Sheriff.

"Jacob is rigging a makeshift bridge for us to get across the road. We walked far enough to see the edge of where the mansions are located. Too bad we can't bring the trucks in… but hey, that's a bridge we'll cross another day."

"Okay, we're gonna head up to the edge of town. We should be in position about 5:30 pm…," said DJ.

"We're grabbing a quick" … DJ cut off mid-sentence, "DJ, someone's coming," Gage hissed, barely above a whisper!!

In a flash, the boys shoved their bikes behind the nearest building – the old Livery. Ten seconds later, a Can-Am came flying down the road. But, this wasn't just any model – it was a Can-Am Maverick. Fast. Much faster than the Defender they saw last week.

"Holy shit, Sheriff, that was close." "Are you still there?" asked DJ. He turned the volume way down and put in his earpiece!

"DJ, are those guys there?" asked the Sheriff. DJ looked around, and the boys and their bikes pressed as close as they could to the wall.

"Yeah, let me check it out, I'll get back to you in a few minutes," said DJ. He snuck up to the corner of the Livery, peeked around it, and saw that the Can-Am was over by the school. They were loading in what appeared to be the last bit of stolen goods into the Maverick.

The Maverick didn't have much storage, so they were clearly prioritizing the smaller, valuable items.

DJ waved the boys over and asked them to come up to him. "They're packing up, heading out in a few minutes," said DJ. "We're gonna give them a head start before we move." They all quickly looked down the street, then ducked back behind the Livery.

DJ pointed to the road. DJ believed the road to the Mansions curved past the school, then up a slight hill and around one final corner. They obviously were hauling in more stolen goods from the past robberies and then packing them into one of the mansions.

"Hey DJ, I never asked before, are they hoping to catch these guys and take them to jail tonight," asked Gage.

DJ didn't answer that question just yet. "Hey guys, get ready to move your bikes against this wall, depending on if they leave or stay for a bit, said DJ. He wasn't sure if they were moving straight out or going to stay for a while.

The boys walked back and forth between the back and the front of the Livery. They were focused on peering around the corner, when all of a sudden, ANOTHER Can-Am showed up, opposite the direction of the Maverick. This one was the Defender, the one they saw last week, that could haul a lot more stuff.

"They're obviously clearing out of here," said DJ. Logan noticed that Gage and Charlie were getting brazen when looking over at them.

"Let's get back," said Logan. "If they look over here, they could see us, and the whole thing is blown"!

Now 5:10 pm, they were a little behind, and the boys had to get a move on to keep schedule; they were going into a new territory they had zero idea what it looked like, and they had to do most of it in the dark. They headed out, about half to three-quarters throttle. From maps they had looked at, they had about 20 minutes of riding, and one hill to push up before getting into "Silver Mine Estates."

"DJ, come in," said the Sheriff. "HEY GUYS, STOP"!! DJ raised his arm, and they came to a quick stop.

"I'm here, Sheriff, what's up?" said DJ. By now, all the bikes were turned off.

"We have a problem, actually a pretty big problem," said the Sheriff, in an exasperated tone.

"They put up a laser trip that alerts them when someone is coming."

DJ had his earpiece in, so the boys couldn't hear what was said. They just knew he was shaking his head like "What now?"

"We just happened to see it with night vision when we happened to walk up the road a little bit," said the Sheriff.

"Even though they think there is no way in from the other direction…chances are, you have a laser trip wire set up for your direction as well. So, make sure you have your night vision goggles on!"

"Hey Sheriff, I have an idea. Let me talk it through with the team," said DJ.

"Okay, over and out for now," said the Sheriff. DJ explained the new obstacle, and it was a big obstacle. Nothing seemed easy!

DJ explained it to the boys, and they could definitely get around the laser trip… But getting the Sheriffs down the road….an entirely separate problem!

"Alright, here's the deal. There might be another laser trip ahead for us,

PLUS, could be another one coming from the Sheriff's direction. We might be able to sneak around it if we can spot it. But getting the Sheriff and his team past it? Not gonna happen."

Logan spoke up. "So … what if instead of the Sheriff going to them … we make them come to the Sheriff?"

DJ's eyes lit up. "That's exactly what I was thinking," said DJ!

Gage and Charlie seemed perplexed with the whole plan, or maybe they didn't want to understand it!

"Wait…so we bait them into chasing us down the road, and then when they are close to the Sheriffs…you guys catch them coming the other way," asked Gage.

"Exactly," said both DJ and Logan at the same time!

"HEY, it's not perfect, but given these new facts, I don't see how we have any other choice," said Logan.

"Logan, you're gonna make a hell of a detective one day," exclaimed DJ! He paused for a minute before moving on..he was realizing that he was putting the boys in harms way. He knew these guys were armed, and if something happened, he could never live with himself.

"DJ you ready," asked Logan. "Yeah, I'm good," said DJ. "Okay, so we have to watch the road like hawks," said DJ, as he and Logan put on his night vision goggles to ride.

"Okay I have to go a little ahead with the night vision, because the headlights from the bikes will knock out the night vision" said DJ.

They pulled out slowly at first, until DJ got comfortable riding with the night vision. It was about a half mile to the mansions from the main street of Silver Mines. DJ raised his arm, and everyone came to a stop. He walked forward, and sure enough, a laser trip was on the road. He had seen these before in the military.

"Hey Sheriff, come in," said DJ. "Sure, enough we found the laser trip"! Before Sheriff could answer, they all looked for a way around.

"Okay, let's walk the bikes around this," said DJ. "I'll give them credit we would've blasted right through it if we didn't have a warning"!

They had one stream to go through, but if the Can-Ams could go through, they could go across without any problem. But that water was pretty deep and cold! DJ kept his night vision on just in case there was another laser trip.

Now, at 5:30 pm, they came around what was the last turn, a slight hill, and then, they should see the bridge over to the mansions. The roads were almost exactly what they were expecting, even the hill.

Now it was getting dark, and was going to get even darker, as the night wore on. "Okay, let's start pushing, this is what the training was for boys," said DJ.

"When we get to the top, we have a decision to make," said DJ. When we get to the bridge, do we take the bikes over the bridge, or leave them behind?

"I think we do the latter," said Logan. The boys kept pushing and were almost to the top.

"I think you are right," said DJ.

"Okay, let's keep it quiet," said Logan. It was now Logan's wish he, too, had a gun, but the Sheriff said no every time Logan had asked.

As they rounded the corner leading into Silver Mines Estates, they could see the street surrounded by beautiful, and huge mansions on either side of the street. They could not make out all of the houses, which they believed were six houses, three on both sides of this magnificent street!

DJ quickly showed them a hiding spot for the bikes, and it was cold enough to keep their helmets on. DJ and Logan put on their night vision goggles, with Gage and Logan keeping their hands-on DJ and Logan's shoulders. They quickly walked down one street to look around.

The oak trees were huge, and because of the rain in Montana, these houses from the 1920s had lawns. They ran the infra-red lights up and down one of the homes. Truly, these homes were incredible. Both Logan and DJ shared their lights with Gage and Charlie so they could see the trees and the homes.

It was so eerie and quiet, with no street lights or lights on inside the homes. The trees still had leaves on them, and with the wind blowing, the leaves were coming off the trees, just like back home in Clear Springs.

The new plan was understood…the boys and DJ knew they would soon have to go inside a home… or more than one home, to find these guys!

Then, make the getaway to have these goons chase them?! What could go wrong!?

"Okay, we're gonna go around the back of this first house," whispered DJ.

"I really have no idea which house to start with... it may start from here as well, hands on shoulders, here we go!"

It was crazy. Here was a street of six huge, beautiful mansions that have not been lived in for what seemed like a lifetime.

Fortunes made…fortunes lost!

The wind was blowing slightly, and wolves howled in the distance. They were about to walk into a supposedly haunted mansion—or worse, a house with known criminals! Or both!!

They got to the back door, and it was locked. How could it be locked?

"Okay, I'm gonna go to the front door, see if it's open, and I will walk back to open the door," said DJ.

"That seems crazy, DJ, but okay, we're not going anywhere," whispered Gage.

It seemed like a lifetime waiting for DJ! The boys kept their heads on a swivel, not saying a word. About two minutes later, DJ rustled with the door and opened it, just like you would with your back door to your house. The door was heavy; you could tell these homes were made with incredible quality!

"Okay, boys, I don't think this is their hideout house, but wow, you cannot believe this place," exclaimed DJ. "Come in, welcome to my ghost house," said DJ. Somehow, that did not seem hilarious to the boys, but he was trying to make it a little lighter…he knew they were scared out of their minds.

Right now, this whole trip doesn't seem like a great idea to the boys. DJ was worried too…and you could hear it in his voice!

CHAPTER 10

What's for Dinner Max?

DJ shined his light into the kitchen at the left. Directly in front of them was the entrance to the living room, dining room, and the most incredible spiral staircase! A beautiful chandelier was directly above them as they walked through to the staircase.

The floors were only slightly tattered, pictures still on the walls, furniture in place, well, mostly in place, with amazing woodwork on the staircase and stairs leading upstairs. Both Logan and DJ shared their lights and their infrared glasses so Charlie and Gage could see what they were seeing.

They moved like shadows—silent, deliberate. Not a single footstep echoed. The quiet was almost unsettling, suggesting the house was likely empty. But still, they took no chances. This place was more amazing than they ever expected!

As DJ led them upstairs, a faint creak echoed from somewhere near the kitchen – maybe a cupboard or a door slowly opening. All eyes shifted, except DJ's. He kept moving, gaze locked on the stairwell.

"Look, I'll take Charlie and go this way, you take Gage and go towards the front bedrooms," whispered DJ to Logan.

They split. Gage clung tightly to Logan's shoulder—not just touching it, but hanging on. The Howlers had been terrifying, but this? This was something else entirely,

Logan and Gage made it into the front room, and they shared their earbuds to listen for DJ. Instead of yelling "clear" when they went into a room, they decided to knock on the wall three times. "Knock, knock, knock" was DJ in the back rooms. Logan did the same. There were four, maybe five, bedrooms upstairs.

Still being quiet, the boys made a careful search. "Alright, nothing here." said DJ. Let's head to the next house. He led the way downstairs, moving quickly."

"DJ, slow down," Charlie whispered. "We can't see what you are seeing!"

They moved methodically and quietly walked to the back door of mansion. Before stepping outside, they paused, checking for any signs of movement.

No chances were taken, they peered carefully out the door before they walked out of the house.

They reached the back door of the second mansion in less than a minute, which also was locked. Without explaining, DJ made his way to the front door, again, this front door was unlocked.

Within seconds, DJ made it to the back door, and this time, it had a louder creak as he pushed. They opened it slowly and carefully. DJ looked for his pistol before stepping inside. This mansion seemed somewhat similar, maybe a tad smaller, but the floors were in great shape, with more furniture, pictures on the walls, and an even more beautiful spiral staircase.

They went back to the kitchen and found food, water, and other provisions! Someone had clearly been living there—maybe still was.

"Okay, we move slowly, and if they are upstairs, be ready to run out the door and to the bikes," whispered DJ.

"Great," whispered Charlie, who was freaked out at this point!

They moved up together now, up the staircase and into the master bedroom. The room was immaculate. Beautiful furniture, perfectly arranged, like a snapshot from before everything changed. These bedrooms were spectacular, the beds, the furniture, everything was still in its place. Chances are, people took what they could when they lost their homes.

Against the wall, they found some of the stolen goods. Someone had slept in this room – sheets rumpled, toiletries in the bathroom like someone left for a quick errand. It could've passed for a boutique hotel. If this were a hotel, what a beautiful hotel! They could hear sounds and felt like someone was whispering, but everyone's imaginations were at their very highest in a house like this…you could hear the house creak and moan.

"Okay, guys, we have to keep moving. Let's check the other bedrooms," said DJ. The room was immaculate—beautiful furniture, perfectly arranged, like a snapshot from before everything changed. People must've grabbed what they could when fleeing, but much here had been left behind.

No one knew what these noises were until Gage said, "Hey, this place is haunted!"! No one said otherwise. There was no other reason for these kinds of noises. No one argued.

"LOOK, LOOK," Charlie hissed, pointing across the street.

"There is someone outside the house, smoking." The boys all looked out the window, and sure enough, they saw someone outside smoking…now two guys smoking.

"Nice catch, Charlie," exclaimed DJ, no longer quiet.

"Okay, guys…you know what we do next, YES?" The boys kept looking out the window.

"Hey, Sheriff, come in," said DJ. "Are you there?"

"Yes, we're here, DJ," said the Sheriff.

"We're all in position, Jacob did a great job in getting us across the river, or stream…whatever you want to call it." The boys kept their eyes on the goons down the street.

"We located the offenders, well, Charlie located them," said DJ. "They are two houses down on the opposite side, so we're gonna

BAMM, BAMM!!

The sound cracked through the silence like gunfire. The chandelier overhead swayed violently. The Sheriff was still on the phone. "WHAT THE HELL IS THAT NOISE DJ," asked the Sheriff.

"YOU GUYS OKAY?" The boys didn't move or say a word, they just looked at each other. "DJ DJ?"

"Sheriff, I have to call you back. I have no idea what that was, but we're okay… for now." DJ hung up the phone, and they all moved to the door. The air inside buzzed with tension. Something – someone-had made that deafening noise. And now … a chilling shhhhh floated through the room.

But nothing had crashed down. Only the chandelier was swaying, and now…there was a swishing type of sound, as if someone was saying "shussshhhh" to someone.

"Okay, let's get out here, and I'll tell you the plan," said DJ. "Can we use flashlights now, DJ," Gage's voice trembled, clearly, he and Charlie in particular, were spooked out of their minds!

"No!! No flashlights," said DJ.

"Let's just get out of here. The boys looked around the house, and the chandelier continued to sway, but now just a little less. The stairs creeped as they went down.

As they approached the back door, as fast as they could in the dark, they heard someone talking as if they were coming up the walk.

"SHITTTT, they're coming inside," DJ whispered!!

They did not have time to reach the back door! No time to escape. To the right of the massive foyer was a door. Not knowing what the room was, they all ducked into the dining room…an absolutely beautiful and grand room. They all walked in and got stealth quick!! DJ reached to make sure his radio was off.

The dining room table remained intact, with only a few chairs missing. The table was massive, and at one time, long ago, it held dinner for 10 people or more.

The front door opened, and Bob, Larry, and a third person walked in. DJ could see him, and although it was dark, he could make out their faces with their flashlight. "It didn't look like Max," DJ said to himself.

That day alone, there were TWO close calls. "Larry, look, look, the chandelier's moving again, like the other day," said Bob. DJ knew Bob's deep voice by now.

"That crazy light, look at it move," said the third voice, in a thick Russian accent.

Bright flashlights were moving all around the living room and foyer as they walked back to the kitchen. "Soon these goods will be moved, and we get you guys paid," said the Russian!

"This place will be phenomenal for the next set, particularly when we move the guns up here," said Larry. DJ couldn't believe what he was hearing; his heart pounded. Gun running? They were going to be gun-running up here?! Is that why the Russian was there?

"Okay, new plan! Let's grab our stuff and get back over…the tri-tip should be done," said Bob. "I can't wait to sleep in a bit…with the ghosts, haha"! DJ waited till they were clearly out the door and down the walk, just in case they came back in the door.

"Okay, well…I don't know what the hell that was…but holy crap, let's keep moving," said DJ. He turned his flashlight on but pointed it towards the floor, but could at least have eye contact with the boys.

"Let's plan on getting out of here," said DJ.

The boys sprinted through the dark to the back door, when there was a loud thump behind the wall in the foyer, and a faint hissing noise from the ceiling area came almost simultaneously! Like a 'thump- thump hissssss'!

Let's get the hell out here," said Charlie, in a scared and not so quiet tone! Without another word, they filed out the back door!

"Sheriff, come in," said DJ. "I'm here, you guys okay," asked the Sheriff. "You scared the crap out of us"! DJ walked over to the door to make sure no one was there.

"Okay, we'll tell you all about it when we see you in a bit," said DJ. "But right now, you need to know we believe there are FOUR people in their group…at least….and definitely two we believe are Russian"!

Chloe was sitting in the truck with Jacob, Bobby, and Travis. Chloe was listening over the radio and she started crying. "What in the world is going on?" said Sheriff. It was beginning to sound like a mob movie!

Sheriff Joe and the Deputies were also in the trucks staying warm, but they had the Can-Am's over the temporary bridge, ready to go, thanks to Jacob and the boys helping him build it in less than an hour. No way this bridge would hold their trucks, but getting people over and the Can-Am's, not a problem!

"Let's get these boys and DJ out of here," said Sheriff. "Maybe we can make the diner in Kalispell before 11 pm." Sheriff didn't care about making the diner, but he did want this over, SOON!

DJ rallied the boys. "Guys, we're at the end. We're gonna walk the bikes behind the first home. Then sneak behind house #3. I go in the back door. They'll be eating." said DJ.

"Wait, DJ," said Gage. "What if we wait in the street and let them chase us?" DJ looked at Logan, "Tell them why, Logan." Logan looked at his brother.

"Because, if we wait for them, they will know something is up," said Logan!

"BUT….DJ, I'm re-thinking this chase idea," said Logan. "That Maverick they have is going to fly…it's way faster than our bikes,"! DJ knew he had to calm the boys down, including Logan, the one he could always count on to be cool and collected!

"I already thought about that," said DJ. "We're gonna reach the bikes before they reach the Maverick, trust me."

"How far do we go for the intercept?" asked Gage. "Is it still"??

"About a mile," said DJ as he interrupted Gage. So, grab a quick drink, a piece of jerky," and let's go interrupt their tri-tip dinner," said DJ, as he fists pumped the boys. They finished in less than 30 seconds. They took one look towards the door to make sure the coast was clear. By now they had forgotten about the loud bang they heard earlier, and, the supposed ghosts.

To the boys…there was no "supposed" about the ghosts they heard earlier!

"Hey, Jacob, are you still comfortable with everything?" asked the Sheriff. Jacob knew Chloe was scared to death. After all, she had just heard that the boy she had a major crush on was drawing out known criminals…that now involved a Russian!! "Yeah, I'm good, Sheriff." Let's get in position. Chloe couldn't help but tear up…the boy she loved was in danger!

They moved their Can-Am's into the middle of the road. The two Sheriffs were lined up in front, with the Deputies Can-Am slightly behind. Jacob was in his pickup on the other side of the makeshift bridge with Chloe, Travis and Bobby, watching…taking it all in.

"Okay, we're ready when you're ready, DJ," said the Sheriff. "Tell me when you're ready, DJ, and I will say 'GAME TIME!"

The boys pushed their bikes down behind house #1. They positioned their bikes to make a fast getaway. DJ and Logan had their infrared lights on, goggles down. They made it across a small set of bushes to get to house #2.

Big problem…they could not cross thru the backyard from house two, to get to house #3.

It started to make more sense to the boys. It was absolutely critical they understood the plan, and didn't question what DJ was laying out to the boys!

"We're gonna walk right in the back door of their house, and we're gonna sneak in," said DJ. "THEN, they are going to see us, I make a loud noise to run…and we run to the bikes as FAST as you can to the bikes!"

"This is how they are going to chase us!!"

The boys nodded, and even though they could not see each other, DJ could see the outline of them nodding, and he knew they were on board!

DJ took one last look at the boys. "Sheriff, be ready, here we go," said DJ in a gruff, whispered plan. Both Sheriffs and the deputies moved into position on the Can-Am's. Jacob, along with Chloe, Bobby and Travis waited in the warm truck.

DJ led the way, the boys in line, hands on shoulders, as they headed to the front door. "DJ, we hear you!" Sheriff's voice rang over the radio.

"IT'S GAME TIME," said the Sheriff!

As DJ and the boys approached the back door, a faint murmur of voices drifted through the walls. Just outside the backdoor was their bar-b-cue, still hot with charcoal. The food smelled amazing!

DJ carefully opened the knob on the door, being super careful not to make any creeks or groans! They opened the door so so quietly, to not make any noise!

Halfway through the threshold, the voices became clearer—Max and his associates were deep in conversation. The glow of the dining room light spilled into the hallway, casting long shadows. The house's layout mirrored the one they'd narrowly escaped from earlier, adding to the tension.

 DJ and the boys were now inside by the back door, which led into the kitchen. "Okay, let's go over the plans before tomorrow," said Max to Dmitrius, what are tomorrow's plans with the guns?"

DJ raised his fist, signaling the others to halt. They listened intently. "Tomorrow, you get paid," said Dmitrius.

"And tomorrow, we offload these things, and in a separate truck, we bring in the next shipment"!

Everyone was listening to these guys, including DJ and the boys. Both Dmitrius and Max talked in a thick Russian accent.

"And every couple of days, we off-load truck," said Dmitrius. "Then bring truck up highway, and then off to Boise." Not one of the boys moved….no one talked.

DJ motioned for the group to move cautiously toward the kitchen's rear, aiming to avoid the dining room where the men were eating. The plan was to navigate through the back of the kitchen, into the living room, and then, out the front door.

This was ridiculous, very dangerous and extremely scary!

Dmitrius, Max, Bob and Larry were now back to being loud! The boys walked single file, following DJ into the room by the front door.

There was no admiring this house. The living room was dim, illuminated only by the faint light from the dining room. DJ approached the front door, easing it open. He signaled for Charlie to approach first, followed by Gage and Logan.

As Gage neared the front door, the floor did a loud CREEK! Everyone stopped. The problem was, they were not in position the way DJ wanted them to be, to be totally safe.

Dmitrius and his gang also stopped talking. "Hey…we have ghooostss back," said Max in his thick Russian accent, "I wonder if they swing from big light again," laughed Dmitrius and his boys, in his thick Russian accent!

"Take a look, Dmitrius"!

Dmitrius rounded the corner, his expression one of confusion and surprise.

DJ, seizing the moment, drew his Sig Sauer P-320 and shouted, "RUNNNNN." DJ yelled as LOUD as he could! The boys ran out the door, followed by DJ. Gage and Logan surged ahead, leaving Charlie struggling to keep up. "LET'S GO CHARLIE," yelled Logan!

They made it to the bikes, threw on their helmets…no strapping them on at this point! DJ looked back to see where they were at, and Dmitrius was the closest. The bikes all started, and they started moving out, FAST!

As Charlie started his bike, Dmitrius grabbed his handlebars. "HELPPPPP," yelled Charlie! DJ turned around, laid his bike down! He yelled at Dmitrius…HEY!! Dmitrius swung around to look at DJ, and DJ flat knocked him down with one punch!

There was a small "thud" as Dmitrius hit the ground! "GOOOOO CHARLIE," yelled DJ. "GOOOOO Charlie," again yelled DJ. Charlie was clearly stunned! They could hear one of the Can-Am's closing fast, and DJ assumed the fast Can-Am was coming soon, too!

Dmitrius was laying in the way of Charlie riding off, so DJ quickly moved him aside, mounted his bike, and yelled for the boys to take off!

The road was horrible and full of potholes. Gage led the pack, and the boys were flying, trying to keep up. Both of their Can-Am's were now taking chase, and they were getting closer! DJ predicted they had about 1/4 mile to go, and they were about 100 yards behind…and closing quick!

"DJ, WE HEAR YOU," yelled the Sheriff into his radio. "IT'S GAME TIME EVERYONE"!! Everyone got ready,

"God, please keep the boys safe," Chloe prayed aloud, her voice trembling with emotion.

The boys were flying as best they could over the road. DJ guessed they were 150 yards out from the Sheriff. He turned around, their Can-

Am's were closing very fast! Suddenly, both of their Can-Am's slammed on the brakes.

They realized it was a trap!!

"HIT THE SPOTLIGHTS," YELLED DJ into his microphone. The bikes made way for the Sheriff's Can'Am's speed to take off and chase. The boys and DJ flipped their bikes around and took off after the Can-Am's.

THE PLAN WAS WORKING, UNFOLDING AS HOPED…at least so far! The potholes were tough on the Can-Ams, so the bikes passed all the Can-Ams, with DJ now leading the way. Max's Can-Am Maverick had a good 200-yard head start and was almost out of sight. DJ flew over the bridge and headed toward the house where they were before. Both Sheriffs and the Deputies in their Can-Ams were right behind. They came back over the bridge into the Estates, this time with full headlights and spotlights blasting!

They didn't see Max and his gang at first. DJ and the Sheriffs had their spotlights out, searching everywhere. All of a sudden, they heard their Can-Am's take off into the woods. This could only mean that there was another way out of the Estates and back into who knows where!

DJ started to chase them, but then he and the Sheriffs thought better of it!

"Hold up," the sheriff said. "We can't chase them; they're too fast, and there are too many places to hide. Let's check the houses."

"Needless to say…great job boys," said Sheriff. "DJ…fantastic job"!

Logan went back to give Chloe a ride into the mansions. Gage gave his pop a ride in, and Bobby and Travis went in one of the Can-Am's with the Deputy. That was the least the Sheriffs could do is let them see these crazy mansions.

Chloe rushed to Logan, enveloping him in a tight hug before hopping onto his bike. "Oh my god, I've never been so scared," she exclaimed, her voice shaking. She embraced each of the boys, including DJ, expressing her gratitude.

"Sheriff, can I suggest we split up, I will take the dinner house with the deputies, and Logan and the guys can direct you in the other house," said DJ. "That works for me," said the Sheriff.

DJ led them into the house where they were having their tri-tip dinner, and now that they could have their spotlights on, the detail in these homes was amazing! They all introduced themselves to each other, and they started on the bottom floor. "That dinner actually STILL smells amazing… pretty mean of you guys to interrupt their dinner, DJ," laughed one of the deputies.

"Yeah, well, the two times we came across these fellers, they were bar-b-cueing," said DJ. "While we were eating jerky and bars"! The deputies were blown away with what they were looking at in these homes.

"Oh, by the way, not sure if you believe this or not, but these homes are supposedly haunted," said DJ. "And if you heard what we heard…saw what we saw… in the other house, you would not think I'm crazy"!

They started walking up the grand spiraling staircase, which had a beautiful railing with incredible detail! At the top of the stairs, they turned into the first bedroom—and were instantly stunned. Piled on the bed and stacked on the floor was a staggering number of stolen items. Among the loot were at least 20 rifles, and probably again that number of pistols glinting ominously under the flashlight beams.

Jewelry of all kinds sparkled from open boxes, while at least 10 laptop computers sat neatly in a row, as if waiting to be used. There were also countless other valuables: watches, cameras, wallets, and personal items clearly taken from multiple victims.

In the other bedroom… 15 rifles, pistols, even an antique sword…Stolen from different families' gun cases!! The deputies, including DJ, couldn't believe what they were seeing tonight, between the stolen goods and the house!

"Okay, let's take pics, bag and tag it," said DJ.

In the other house, Logan, Gage & Charlie were showing the two Sheriffs and Jacob around. They also couldn't believe what they were seeing…the details, the beautiful chandelier, the spiraling staircase! "Guys, this could be a whole, beautiful brand-new city," exclaimed the Sheriff!

As they walked around taking it all in, Logan held Chloe's hand up the stairs, Logan telling Chloe about the swaying chandelier just a bit earlier. They walked into the front bedroom where Charlie had seen the goons across the street. Logan left the door open, even he was still a little spooked about this place…and Chloe held onto Logan's arm as tight as she could!

"Logan," Chloe began, her voice barely above a whisper, "I've never been so scared for—"

Before she could finish, Logan turned to her, heart pounding, and kissed her. Their first real kiss.

WHAAMMMM!!

The door slammed shut and then vibrated as if someone was trying to open it!! Logan shined the light towards the door. There was a faint noise that sounded like fingernails on a chalkboard. At the same time, a "shush" sound came out, with a trace of what looked like smoke coming into the light, and just as quickly…, it was gone!

CHLOE SCREAMED AS ABSOLUTELY LOUD AS SHE COULD!!

Logan stood there at first, also trembling, shining his light towards the door.

"HEY YOU GUYS OK," yelled the Sheriff, as he swung the door wide open! "Yeah, we're fine', said Logan. "Sheriff, I swear to you…that door was open, and then it slammed shut," said Logan in a loud voice.

By then, everyone was at the door. ***"Logan…look…the chandelier,"*** said Gage. The chandelier was once again swaying, this time a little less than before. "I'm just glad you guys saw this," said Logan!

Chloe was still shaking, hanging onto Logan's arm. By now, they had forgotten that kiss. "DJ, how you guys coming along over there?" said the Sheriff. "I talked to the Sheriff Joe, he wants his deputies to bag and tag, and see if these guys show up later…they're prepared to stay the night if needed."

"Can we go eat," asked DJ. Sheriff just smiled, he knew these guys had to be starving. "Hey, there is a diner 15 min away," said Sheriff Joe. "I can call them and tell them to stay open, I know the owner."

You didn't have to ask the boys twice! They loaded the bikes in less than five minutes, and in less than ten minutes, they were out! You didn't have to ask Chloe if she wanted to leave. As excited as she was to see these haunted mansions…she was over it now!

Now midnight, as they settled in for dinner, the deputies back at the mansions were calling Sheriff Joe. "Wait, guys, let me put the phone on speaker," said the Sheriff. Bob and Larry came back. Must've been trying to get out of the cold. We heard the door open, cut the lights, waited… they walked right upstairs, and… we've got them in custody!"

Cheers erupted at the dinner. What a finish to the night. "Hey guys, great job," said Sheriff Don.

"Are they going to give up Dmitri and Max"? The Deputy opened the car door. "I don't want to talk in front of them, but I think we'll find out tomorrow," said the Deputy.

The sheriffs, DJ, and Jacob stood and raised their glasses in a toast. Chloe joined them with a huge smile.

"YES! LET'S TOAST TO THE MOTO BOYS…"

The sheriffs, DJ, and Jacob stood and raised their glasses in a toast.

Chloe joined them with a huge smile.

DJ and the boys looked at each other, obviously proud of how they had helped the Sheriffs and the families of their town. Food never tasted so good!

CHAPTER 11

Thank You Montana Chronicle

By the next morning, Bob and Larry had both "lawyered up." Unsurprisingly, they hadn't given up any information about Dimitri and Max, the other two criminals. On the upside, the stolen goods from the mansions had been recovered and brought back to the Sheriff's station, but for now, they had to be held as evidence.

To no one's surprise, Bob & Larry pleaded "not guilty" to their charges, and, were released on bail. There bail was $15,000, and the Sheriff was surprised they got the money so quickly!

Several articles in the newspapers, both in print and online, started causing chaos in Clear Springs and Whisperings Pines. Tourists flooded into town, crowding the diner and eager to try and see Silver Mines and the mansions! Easier said than done...but nevertheless, people wanted to try and get up there!

If Bob & Larry had made it up there using the backroads, others could too. That meant one thing: the roads needed to be fixed – fast. The trouble was, the area's dense woods, winding mountain trails, then so could other would-be adventure seekers.

So, first things first, time to fix all the roads they know that lead into Silver Mines and the mansions. Unfortunately, because of the mountains, woods, and trails, there were so many ways that eventually get you up to the ghost town. And if you know the way there…you can find the mansions!

Meanwhile, robberies continued across the western U.S. The sheriffs now suspected the stolen goods weren't being stashed in the mountains anymore. Instead, they were likely moving straight from the crime scene into multiple getaway vehicles—two, maybe three trucks.

Back in the diner, a different kind of trouble was brewing. A big "No Cell Phones" sign hung prominently inside, but newcomers didn't seem to care. They were completely ignoring the sign at the Diner, "Thank you for not using your cell phone while in the diner." Saturdays were always busy. Two weeks ago, was the trip up the mountain for the Moto Boys, and this Saturday, there was an hour- long wait for diner.

In the back corner of diner, a group of eight people, clearly not from around town, was seated in the back corner – loud phone, obsessed, and ignoring the rules. Jim and Brenda, owners of the diner, were always around for dinner at the diner, walking around and greeting customers. Their family had started the diner over 25 years ago, and had expanded the diner twice over that period of time.

"Hey folks, welcome. I'm Jim - the owner of the diner," introduced Jim. "I think you guys are all new here, and we actually have a sign up that says "no cell phones at the table, so we would really appreciate it if you would turn them off, and put them away while here with us. Can you do that please"?

The table got very quiet, and they all just stared at Jim. "Guys, I am asking nicely," said Jim. "That the dumbest rule I've ever heard," muttered one of the older guys at the table, prompting laughter from his friends sitting next to him. Most of the other guys just snickered, shaking their head in agreement.

And they went back to their phones. Clearly ignoring Jim!

Jim was one of the nicest guys in the world, but particularly given how busy they were tonight, he did not need to put up with this crap. Jim's patience, especially on a packed night, had its limits.

"All I did was ask nicely, and I, THE OWNER, can refuse service to anyone I want here," said Jim in a much louder and irritated tone.

This caught the attention of DJ and the boys who were having dinner at the same time.

"So, either put the damn phones away or get the hell out – I really don't care anymore.," said Jim. "If you don't like the rules, please, go somewhere else! Should I keep your dinner order going, or, should I cancel it"?

"Billy, let's put them away, we're hungry," said one guy half-heartedly. Still, no one moved, at least yet. "Okay, Jim, your diner, your rules, we don't want to have the deputy and his moto geeks get involved," said Billy. All of his buddies laughed super loud. Jim looked over at DJ, and DJ gave a subtle signal to just let it go.

Gage, however, was fuming as their attitude pissed him off in particular. "Who the hell are these guys," asked DJ. Everyone in the diner felt very uneasy! By that time Jim had walked away and was clearly mad at the situation. He walked by DJ and the boys' booth, saying quietly, "hey, I hope they pull out their phones again…I'll just kick them out," said Jim!

This group clearly knew enough about the Moto Boys and DJ from articles online to make stupid comments. "Guarantee we would smoke these geeks in a race," Billy scoffed. "I'm surprised their mommy and daddy let them go up the mountain"! This made all of his buddies at the table laugh super loud.

DJ had heard it, and it was enough for him.

"Hey jackasses - shut the hell up," he said loud enough for nearby tables to hear. "No one here gives a rats ass what you idiots think, everyone here is trying to spend a good time having dinner."

Jim heard all of this. He grabbed their food that had just come up, he packaged it up to go, and delivered it to the table. "I've heard enough. Dinner is on me. Finish your beer, and get out…plastic silverware's in the bag!"

The diner applauded Jim's move, and you could tell this irritated and embarrassed Billy. "Y'all are a bunch of sensitive babies," said Billy. "Like I said, we would crush you guys in a race"!

Now Logan had heard enough. He guessed these guys were about 21 years of age. "Well big boy, we're riding tomorrow, put your big boy pants on, let's see just how fast you guys are," challenged Logan. "Or did your mommy let you bring your bikes?" DJ motioned back at Logan and Gage to get them to cool it.

"We know where you ride, see ya tomorrow…say 10 am," said Billy on the way out. "Perfect, see you there," Logan said, smiling.

Billy's group pulled phones out on the way out, filming patrons in the diner, a sign of total disrespect. "They'll never, and I mean never, be invited back," said Jim, to customers slight applause.

"Hey guys, no harm, no foul, but you show strength by not getting into it with them," said DJ. "Besides, I have a couple of questions for them…we have new information from the Sheriff and other Sheriffs in the county, and our Sheriff, and I, want to go over it with all of you tomorrow night, at the station."

It was a perfect day for riding, a rare sunny 40 degrees, and with the rain that happened earlier in the week, a beautiful loamy dirt with great berms to look forward to riding. Logan didn't say much, but Gage was chatty with a million questions for his brother. Logan just wanted to eat his breakfast.

"Dad are you gonna watch…Logan we need to kick their butts," said Gage waited for his brother to say something, but Logan stayed quiet, clearly focused. "Let's load the bikes," he said at last, not saying anything at this point.

When they got to the track, it almost looked like a race event. DJ was there with his deputy cousin, Sheriff was there. Even Charlie's parents had come. The Sheriff had recently acquired Travis and Bobby's bikes to purchase, so they were there to watch however.

Billy approached Logan's pickup, "Well, it's your track, we'll watch which way to go," said Billy, with a smirk.

"No problem," Logan replied calmly. The boys couldn't help but notice the almost new bikes these guys had; there were 3 guys riding, two Yamaha YZ 250R's, and one Honda CRF 250R…new tires, super clean, and all of them had new riding gear. At least they looked fast and very well prepared! But, it was yet to be proved.

DJ was the first to drop into the track, with Gage, Logan, and Charlie trailing closely. About a half-lap behind, Billy and his two buddies joined the action. As always, Gage and Logan stood on their pegs all the way around the course—just like the pros. Riders like Jett Lawrence and Chase Sexton always warmed up that way, and the boys mimicked their idols to a tee.

On this track, there were great berms in the turns, a small whoop section, with a couple of double jump sections. Only Gage and Logan did the doubles. No doubt the boys would be anxious to see if these guys could do doubles.

After a few laps, Gage moved to the front, followed by Logan. DJ could barely believe how fast they were riding – faster than he had ever seen them ride before, and DJ himself was riding well, but certainly was not jumping the doubles.

Billy, riding one of the new Yamahas, was the fastest in his group. They weren't jumping yet, but their speed was obvious – and so was the fact that their bikes had more power than the Moto Boy's bikes!

They all stopped by the side of the track, turned off their bikes. "We know your name, Billy, who are your two buddies," asked DJ. My name is DJ, this is Logan, Gage, and Travis." Billy pointed at his two guys, "this here is Johnny on the Yamaha, and Braden on the Honda."

"Well, you guys have nice bikes," said Travis. "I thought you guys had bikes too," asked Billy. DJ turned around to make sure Travis didn't tell them what really happened to the bikes.

"Yeah, our bikes just plain wore out and weren't worth replacing, so we're getting new bikes this week, we think," said Travis.

"So, you guys wanted to have some fun and race," said Logan. "Do you want to start off, or follow us?" Billy looked around at his buddies, "go ahead, we'll follow."

"I'll follow you guys," said DJ. "I don't want to get into anyone's way"!

Gage blasted around a berm and launched over the first double, clean and smooth. While it was obvious that Billy and his buddies had unmatched bikes, but on a tight track like this, it didn't matter near as much as it would on a motocross track. Logan could tell that Gage was holding back, to see where those guys were at on the track.

There were no excuses on riding for the new guys, they had enough riding around the track to learn it. When Gage could see they were making ground, Gage turned up the wick, as did Logan. Travis was trying his best, but he was passed by DJ, who was riding well…not as fast as Billy's group though.

Gage and Logan absolutely blew the doors off of Billy and his gang!

After ten laps, Gage had caught up to the back of Johnny and Braden. With their point made, he and Logan pulled off. Billy coasted to a stop behind them, laughing, "Okay, you guys are the real deal," laughed Billy. "Can't imagine what you guys would do on this bike." Gage laughed, "yeah, that would be sweet, but we also do a lot of trail riding…would you like to jump over some logs with us in the woods over there," said Gage, pointing over his shoulder.

"No, we'll stick to the track, but we wouldn't mind riding a little more," asked Billy, now being more respectful than last evening. "Sure, no problem, guys, I have a few questions if you don't mind," asked DJ. The Sheriff was over standing next to the dads talking, wanting to listen in, but didn't want to intimidate anyone.

"Sure, ask away," said Billy. DJ looked around to motion everyone in to listen. "Look I am new to riding, but I've been around long enough to know almost everyone that rides dirt bikes, no matter what type of dirt riding, are good honest guys, just out to have a good time," said DJ.

Billy started to reply, but DJ cut him off. "And I'm not talking about last night. I'm sure if you came back to the diner, you'd be respectful and follow the rules. I believe that."

"In fact, on the way home, we are stopping off to apologize and pay our bill, regardless if we are invited back," said Billy. "My mom would have kicked our asses last night if she were there"!

"Okay, fantastic, that makes me, or us, feel much better," said DJ. "Now here's my question…do you know of a riding group headed up by a guy named Braxton? Someone who has a bad reputation around Whitefish, Kalispell, even Bozeman bars?"

Billy looked down, and without hesitating, "Yep those guys are idiots, and give guys like us a bad name." And his buddies are even worse. They get into fights, and some of them have records. But lately, they have not been around at events like in the past." AND… we don't want it out that we gave you any info"!!

"Why are you asking, what did those jerks do now," asked Billy. Both Johnny and Braden let Billy do all of the talking. "I got into a fight with him last year when he was flirting with my girl," said Billy.

By that time, Billy's girlfriend had come up to the group, as had Chloe, followed by the Sheriff. "The reason we're asking is they might be involved in some thefts in the county," said the Sheriff. "IF they are involved, they aren't riding their motorcycles, as much as we know, and right now, everything is preliminary."

"I do know this much," said Billy. They have dirt bikes, Harleys, and Can Ams. They're decent riders, but not superfast by any means…not like these flyers," laughed Billy. "And nothing but respect, guys, I apologize for being an ass last night"!

"Hey, thanks for the info," said DJ. Let's ride another 20 minutes and get out of here, okay"?

Everyone disbanded back to their respective places to watch, with Gage and Logan taking their place at the front of the track, followed by Billy, Braden, and Johnny. Gage went half speed around the track to start, and then flew thru the whoops, He was the only rider that knew how to "toe-tap" on the beginning of the whoops, as well as whip to keep the height down on the doubles.

After two laps, Gage and Logan were at least a half lap ahead of everyone else. At the end of the riding, they all pulled off the track, shook hands, and said their goodbyes. "Thanks for the lesson in riding…you guys would do very well in racing," said Billy. That really made Gage in particular feel good. But again, he'd never ask his dad to race. He and his brother's live were full, busy, and they suspected the group would become even busier!

The chairs at the Sheriff's office were all out, again. Sheriff wasted no time in getting everyone to sit down. DJ's cousin was back for this meeting, as were the Sheriff and Deputies from Kalispell.

"I'll start off by saying congrats to the boys whooping some butt today at the track," said the Sheriff. "That needed to happen after the Diner incident last night, but I understand that is all behind us."

"Now, let's get into it," said Sheriff. He went around the room introducing everyone again, and then reminded all of them in the room, that this information was not to leave the room, under no circumstances! "The articles that came out about Silver Mines and the Silver Mines Estates created so many problems for us," said Deputy Colton. "From having rogue people now in town, people asking for directions to get up to Silver Mines, loud people camping in the woods, staying up late…we had two noise complaints this week alone…something we never have in our town"!

"But that's not why we have the other Sheriffs here tonight, we've learned the robberies are now extending across several counties, from home, to business and autos," said the Sheriff. "Silver Mines and the mansions were perfect hiding spots until we blew that out of the water," thanks to the Moto Boys and DJ." The other Sheriff's in the room applauded and thanked them!

"The beautiful thing about Montana is the wilderness, the trails and the beauty of our mountains," said the Sheriff. "The bad news for us, is that these trails lead up to abandoned barns and old homes, not unlike Silver Mines," said DJ. "Our Sheriffs informed us of two potential hiding spots to hold a lot of stolen goods."

Logan raised his hand to speak. "What I don't understand is why are they putting the goods in these hiding spots at all," asked Logan. "Sheriff, if you don't mind, can I take this question," asked DJ. Sheriff nodded in approval.

"Great question, and perhaps some of it is going out the house and, on the road," said DJ. "But most is being kept in a hideout for two reasons…one, because less of a chance of getting caught if someone reports the robbery right away, and we are looking for suspicious cars. Secondly, they are most likely laying everything out for their buying parties to figure out how much they will pay for the stolen goods."

"Look, here are the facts," said Sheriff. "These guys are ten moves ahead of us, and they have all of their hiding spots figured out, not to mention, the homes they plan on robbing"!

"I want to make sure we are on the same page, as far as using the Moto Boys," said Sheriff. "In no way, shape, or form can we put them in harm's way, BUT, we can't get this fixed without these guys"!

"So, two, actually three things we need from the boys," said DJ. First, every one of the towns will have their own guy that has a bike, like DJ, where the boys can help get the Deputy up to the hiding spot. In fact, I will be accompanying the new Deputies when the time comes."

"Secondly, we need you boys to help train these guys to ride, and third, help me get new people we expect as early as this week, off the mountain and out of Silver Mines," said DJ. "We cannot take a chance on those towns getting screwed up, them getting hurt, or, causing a fire"!

"Gary, the owner of our local store in town, was questioning a few guys at his store who have dirt bikes; he said they're planning on getting up to Silver Mines this week," said Sheriff.

"It hasn't happened yet, but we're trying to put signs up in a few places, plug holes like the entrance into Silver Mines," but we're on notice that people want to experience these towns…and knowing what we now know, it's not a good idea"!

"If it's okay Sheriff," said Sheriff Joe, "can I tell you what's happening in our town. Similar to your robberies, these guys get in and out, steal the best jewelry, steal guns, they wear masks, and get out quick in case they have alarms on their doors"!

Sheriff Joe looked around to make sure everyone was looking at him. He was a big guy, imposing figure, and like Sheriff Don, you could tell he was good at his job, and cared about his team. "We don't want anyone getting hurt while you are helping us, so just like when you are helping your Sheriff, if anyone wants out at any time, no judgment here…we appreciate the help getting to the hiding spots."

DJ looked at his guys. "The Sheriff already is planning on getting bikes for Bobby and Travis this week, so we are now trying to get two additional bikes this week, can you guys help train the new deputies this week if we get the bikes," asked DJ.

"Of course, whatever is needed, whenever it's needed," said Logan. "Just say when and where, and if someone is trying to get up to Silver Mines, we'll definitely be ready for that trip"!!

"How about this Saturday, Logan," said Sheriff. "I need you guys to go up, get Silver Mines lined up with cameras and motion sensors. Also need the Mansions set up with cameras and signs to 'stay out'"!

"Okay, done," said Logan. They were getting very good at getting up the mountain, and even in bad weather, getting down too. It would be Logan, Gage, Charlie, and Gage for this trip. And if everything worked as hoped, they'd be down that night!

CHAPTER 12

You Look Like You Saw A Ghost

By 10 am on Saturday, the boys and DJ made it up to the Silver Mines. It was a beautiful crisp morning with clouds on the horizon, and the possibility of a storm coming in Sunday afternoon, so they planned to get out this afternoon and home in time for diner.

Logan had a date planned that night with Chloe, and lately, they were enjoying each other's company a lot. DJ had written out a plan for all of the boys, with probably two hours of chores to complete before they could get out of the Estates and down the hill, weather permitting.

DJ gave some lighter chores to all three boys at the mansions, while he did some of the tougher electrical chores that required hidden cameras at the school and the church, so they could catch intruders coming and going!

The work at the mansions required putting signs at each of the mansions, both on the front doors and inside the doors. By 1 pm, the weather was starting to change quickly, and if it continued as it was, no way they would take a chance on getting down the mountain!

The boys were done with four of the six homes, and decided they may as well keep working. "Come in, Logan, can you hear me," radioed DJ on the satellite radio. "I'm here," said Logan. "It's starting to rain pretty good, but it's dries inside the houses. We're taking a break and eating a little lunch"!

"I'm gonna get soaked if I come up," said DJ. "But at least the roads aren't pure mud yet. I'll put on my rain parka and come over now. What house are you guys in right now"?

"Logan can you hear me, what house are you guys in," asked DJ again. Finally, Logan answered but the connection was not great. "We're in number 5," said Logan.

"Oh, you guys in the BIG HOUSE," said DJ. "Ya, I cannot believe how incredible this house is," said Logan. I've never seen a staircase like this in my life!" The outside of this house still looked amazing, and way, way better than the house they were calling "number 4."

Mansion #5 was made from stone, and although it was dirty and somewhat worn, it looked amazing.

And very eerie!

"Okay I will be up there in a few," said DJ. I can't wait to see the inside of that house!"

The boys finished eating at the beautiful dining room table, and decided to look around this house while they waited for DJ to get there. This was the house and the table where they interrupted the Russians having their tri-tip dinner. It was getting dark outside, with the change in weather happening so fast, and it was becoming apparent they wouldn't be going down the mountain tonight. The house had the most incredible chandelier of all the homes, and was probably another 2000 square feet larger than the other homes. In fact, this home had 3 floors, (4 if you count the basement), and…a steam run elevator!

Gage and Charlie went up to the 3rd floor by walking..no one was going to be adventurous enough to try the elevator. The 3rd floor consisted mostly of bedrooms, and all but one of the bedrooms had beds, complete with their own bathrooms and dressers to hold clothes.

They opened one of the dressers, and it actually had a few clothes still in the drawer! "That is beyond creepy," said Charlie. They went down the stairs to floor number 2, and one of the rooms in this massive home had a library, with books still on the shelves!

"Wow, wow, wow," said Gage. "Hey, Logan, get up here and check this out," yelled Charlie. "You won't believe this library"! By the time Logan got up the stairs, a beautiful door was at the far end of the library. Gage opened the door, and shined the light from his phone inside.

It was a long hallway leading to. well, it led somewhere. Gage thought about the house layout; facing the house, he was at the far-right side on the second floor. Did it lead to the other side? The hallway was narrow, and you could see candle holders on both sides of the walls, with most of them empty. It was hard to believe that several that still held candles.

Gage and Charlie were in the hallway, and Logan was at the doorway. "Hey Logan, just in case," said Gage, "put a book at the bottom of the doorway to hold it open. C'mon Charlie, let's go down a little way." Charlie looked and thought about it. He didn't want Gage to think he was a 'scar die cat'. "Okay, but just for a bit," said Charlie. "We have work to do, and I don't want DJ think we're screwing around."

"C'mon, it's fine, we're just going to go a little way," said Gage. Surprisingly, it didn't have much odor. About 200 to 250-feet in, the hallway had a sharp turn to the left. It was getting dark down there, but they had their lights on with their phones. "Charlie, turn your light off," said Gage. "That way we make sure we save your battery, in case mine gets too low."

Charlie turned his off, and then, to be funny, Gage turned his off too. "GAGE. CRAP," yelled Charlie. "C'mon, turn it on, or I am turning mine on"! They were both quiet for a second. Gage accidentally dropped his phone and could hear it bounce for a second. He reached down right away, but couldn't feel it. "Charlie, turn your light on," said Gage, now a little freaked out. "And don't drop it"!! Charlie was shaking now, and hung onto his phone tightly. He opened his cell, and turned the light on, but they didn't see the phone on the floor at first.

"What the hell," said Gage. "Where's the damn phone"! Things were getting weird in a hurry. "Look there it is," said Charlie. "How did it get all the way over there"? It was about 15 feet away. Charlie kept his phone on till he picked it up.

"Wait..Charlie, which way did we go in," asked Gage in a hurried and scared voice. They shined their phone lights in different directions, and each walked no more than 10 feet from one another. They figured they had walked no more than 250 feet…maybe a tad farther, into the hallway. All they wanted at this point was to get OUT!!

"CRAP, this is BAD," said Charlie. "Okay, look, Charlie, let's not panic," said Gage. First, Gage and DJ will look for us and yell. So, I am sure we can go either way and we'll be fine. So…let's just head this way, and one way or the other, we'll get out"!

They headed down the hall, and suddenly, it did not seem like they ame in the same way. They came into a hall with a door. "I think I remember us seeing a door before," said Charlie. "I don't remember ever seeing a door," said Gage, now clearly agitated and upset.

"Let's open the door just to check," said Charlie. "Then let's go back the other way…since we didn't remember this door before." Charlie was scared, but he was a logical, smart kid.

The door opened with a loud creek. It opened into small room, and another door was across the room and to the left. "Okay, I think we go back, we never saw this room before," said Gage. They turned to go back the other way…. suddenly, they heard a faint noise that sounded like wind blowing, almost like a "HISSSS"! "Whoa, what the hell is THAT," asked Gage. "You feel that? On your back"??

Gage didn't say anything, but whispered a faint "yes." They both felt a warm blast of air on their backs, simultaneously hearing this "HISSS" sound! They walked down the hall about 15-20 feet, and now there were TWO ways they could go! "Oh shit," said Gage, looking at Charlie. "We never saw this before, did you Charlie"?!

Charlie didn't say a word. Suddenly, their phone light dimmed!! And then…their lights came back on, but it was faint! They had about 9 percent battery on both of their phones, and keeping the light on was draining their batteries! Charlie started to panic.

"Hey, Charlie," said Gage, almost yelling. "Something…or someone…is MESSING with us! Which way do we go"? Still not saying anything, Charlie thought for a minute and said, "I think we go the other way." They tried to retrace their steps to see if they could tell which way they came…and clearly, they could not figure it out!

"Wait, I think I hear something," said Gage. You hear that"?? Charlie told Gage to shut it. "Gage quiet," said Charlie!! They could hear faint talking, but it didn't sound like Logan or DJ. "Okay, I'm gonna yell," said Gage. By this time, they had one phone on at a time. "LOOOGGAAANNNNN," yelled Gage at the top of his lungs.

They were both stealth quiet at this point. Suddenly, they heard a faint knock that grew louder and louder, faster and faster!!

"KNOCK….KNOCK….KNOCK..KNOCK…KNOCK..

KNOCK...KNOCK…followed by what sounded like someone in slippers walking toward them very fast!

They both turned their lights on, but BOTH were down to less than 5 % of battery on their phones! "SHIIITT" said Gage, "what is going on"!!!

Suddenly, a large BOOM hit the wall near them. Just one loud 'boom'!

"Logan, is that you?" Yelled Charlie. They were hoping, upon hoping, they were messing with them, but they doubted Logan or DJ would do that. This was the scariest either of them had ever been!

Gage's light started going out, and he got down to almost zero battery! "Okay, let's quit standing here, pick a direction, and start walking," said Gage. "Hang onto my sweatshirt," said Gage."We never get separated, especially if we lose our battery."

Charlie started to cry. Gage was trying to hold it together. How could things get this crazy in a period of 5 to 10 minutes?!

Gage and Logan started to walk; they decided to turn the light on for a second, look down the hall, then walk as fast as they could in that direction. They both had one hand hanging onto each other, and the other, straight out in front of them.

Charlie felt something tug on his sweatshirt. "Shit…Gage is that you," asked Charlie, shaking as he asked him! "No, do what," asked Gage. Charlie didn't answer yet, he just kept walking. Charlie never cussed at home…but today seemed necessary to let the words fly!

They walked directly into a wall, or a door! They probably had been walking for about 30 seconds straight, and if you are walking fast, you can cover a lot!

"You gotta be kiddddddddding me," yelled Gage!!! "This is the wrong way…and I'm getting pissed"!! Gage turned his phone on for a second, then the light, and they ran right into a door. And to the right, another door.

"Just how big IS this damn house," said Charlie. "I'm opening both of these doors," said Gage. "Charlie, in just a second, I'm gonna turn off my phone," get your's ready"!

Gage opened the one straight in front of him; it was some kind of a storage room! The room had some crates in the room, a mirror on the wall, and some kind of a dresser. Gage was at 2% battery now. Neither of the boys stepped into the room. They left that door open, and then…. opened the other room.

It was a bedroom?! A bedroom with 3 doors, and on the bed..was a skeleton! "Gage, we gotta go back," said Charlie. "Then make a sharp turn at that hallway, you know what I'm talking about"?

They stared at the skeleton longer than they should have, considering that they had basically no battery left!

"Gage, Logan," yelled DJ. "Where the hell are you guys"?? They could tell it was DJ by his voice. "DJ, can you hear me?" Yelled Gage. DJ CAN YOU HEAR ME!! Both Charlie and Gage were yelling.

The boys could hear DJ yelling but now it was fainter. The boys were banging on the walls, hoping DJ and Logan could hear them. By now they were back in the hallway, trying to decide if they follow one of the other doors in the bedroom, or, the other door in the storage room.

"Gage, we can't hear DJ as well," said Charlie. "So, let's go back the other way." They stood for a second, not knowing what to do. "Yeah, but we never saw that room before," said Gage.

"WHAT'S THAT NOISE?" Said Charlie. They both were super quiet. All of a sudden, they heard a faint scream.

'AAAAAAAAAHHHHHHHHHHHHH……
AAAAAAAAAHHHHHHHHHHHHH……

'AAAAAAAAAHHHHHHHHHHHHH' "Ohhh crap, what is THAT," yelled Gage! The boys were starting to panic, and no one could blame them.

Now they have just started to move, and move fast. They were walking away from where they thought the storage room was, feeling the wall, hanging onto one another. They came to a break in the wall, which told them they could make a turn. "Wait, stop Charlie," said Gage. "Turn your light on."

Charlie had a new cell phone than Gage, and his light was still pretty good, even though he was at 2%. He shined the light both ways, and to the right, it looked like the floor was gone…as if…you would fall down to the next floor…or further! "Well, we aren't going THAT way, said Charlie, now even more panicked.

"OMG, we would have just fallen if we had gone that way," said Gage. That scream they heard before sounded as if it were coming from that hole in the floor, but now it was faint, very faint!

They turned to the left and went down the hall, every ten feet or so, stopping and turning on Charlie's light. After another 20 feet, it turned to the right, and there was another door. They opened it slowly. Another room! But under the door, they could see LIGHT. As in maybe daylight!

"Let's open slowly," said Gage. FINALLY. A room with a window! Both boys looked at each other with a huge smile. But in this room, it was stocked with guns, obviously rifles and pistols that had been stolen! They went to the window and could tell they were on the back side of the house.

"Gage, you see what I see," said Charlie. Look way out there in the woods. You see that"?? Gage looked out, looking everywhere. "All I see are those two deer…WAIT…OMG Charlie!! THE CAN-AM"!?

It was Max's, or one of those guys, Can-Am, that was poorly covered with shrubbery. "Oh my god, does that mean they are here?" Asked Charlie. "I highly doubt it," said Gage. But we'll go out with DJ and Logan and check it out"!

Charlie went to the other door in the room. THIS door was a secret door on the other side. It was a door that was part of a closet!? In other words, there was no way you would ever know it led to the room they were just in…where they found the stolen goods!

. "DJ…LOGAN," yelled Charlie. "DJ…LOGAN," and finally DJ yelled back. "We're coming," yelled DJ back. "Finally," said Charlie.

"That was ridiculous... and no one would believe what we tell them."

"Gage, Charlie…can you hear me?" Said DJ, still not that close. Gage went down the hallway a little bit and yelled, "WE'RE HERRRREEE?" Yelled Gage at the top of his lungs. They could finally hear the footsteps of DJ and Logan, and hear them talking. "Up here," said Charlie.

"Holy crap, I thought we were never gonna find you guys," said Logan. Charlie and Gage looked at each other…" Oh you really have noooo idea," said Gage. We'll tell you about it a little later, but look what we found. Did you guys know this was here"??

Gage and Charlie led them back into the closet and the secret door. It was clear that Max's gang understood this house MUCH better than they did. "I wonder what else is in this house, or how many other hidden rooms were in Mansion #4, or maybe the other homes," said Gage.

DJ and Logan started to walk into the room, mouth's wide open!! "You have GOT to be kidding me," said DJ. They all stood there, started taking pictures, and started counting the watches, the rings…everything!

"Look at the amount of jewelry, the number of Rolex's," said DJ. "Not to mention the number of rifles and pistols, I think could be worth $250,000-$300,000! Maybe more."

"But not worth getting caught," said Logan. "So, my guess is they will send someone else up to try and steal it back," and then go out through the woods…probably a way out we haven't found yet!

"Okay, DJ, check this out," said Charlie. "Great eyes by the way, Charlie," said Gage. "You always see the little things that make a huge difference"! Logan and DJ looked out the window, unable to see it at first. "Oh, now I can see it," said DJ. "My guess is they left it there before, but let's go check it out."

Now, about 5 pm, the thunder, lightning, and rain had stopped, thank god. They all walked out together and started down a small trail in the woods. Before they came down the stairs, they made some "trail marks" in their minds so they could find the Can-Am. They figured it was about 150-200 feet from the house.

They always habitually closed the door they were going out of…just in case a bear wanted to come in and wreak havoc in the house.

They finally reached the Can-Am, and the engine was cold. So, they knew it had been there for a while. Plus, there were leaves on the seats, indicating it had been left there for at least a day, possibly much longer. The key was not in the ignition. "Well, at least they were smart enough to take the key," said DJ. "Actually, I think these guys might be smarter than we give them credit," said Logan. "I think these guys are a couple of steps ahead of us, EVEN though we found their stolen goods."

"Ha, well…I hope you're wrong, Logan," said DJ. "Okay, let's get inside and eat"!

They all knew they were spending the night and decided they would all sleep in the living room, close to one another! They had enough snacks and food for at least one, maybe even two nights.

"Sheriff, come in," said DJ. "Hey, DJ, how's it going, you guys all safe?" Said the Sheriff. DJ paused for a minute and walked away from the group to talk to the Sheriff. "Yeah, we're all good," said DJ. "Gage and Charlie had an adventure that scared the crap out of them..I will tell you more about it later. But…we found a lot...and I mean a LOT of stolen goods that are still here"!

"They also have their Can-Am still here..the one with the truck bed," said Logan. "Tell our mom and dad hi for us, and we'll see them tomorrow"!

Sheriff didn't answer right away. "Sorry DJ," said Sheriff. "Had to walk outside, DC and I are at the Diner with the Dalton's, and DC is outside with me. OH MY GOD, really"?!

I guess we shouldn't be surprised. Well, hide that stuff as best you can; they will return for it at some point. When we get a chance, we'll get it back to the rightful owners. Obviously, they know that house better than we do"!

"We said the same thing," said DJ. "Anyways go back to your dinner, we'll check back after we get our work done in the am…and then back down the mountain."

Being at the diner right now sounded so good right about now. By 7 pm, the stars came out. Fortunately, the water soaked in pretty fast, and as long as it didn't rain in the morning, they would make it down the mountain easily.

After Gage and Charlie's scare, they were glad to be around Logan and DJ. They sat at the table, laughing about the time they interrupted Max's dinner, and how DJ had to pull one of the Russians off of Charlie's handlebars.

Logan and DJ couldn't believe the experience Gage and Charlie had, when they told it back during their 'dinner time'. "DJ, you think you woulda been freaked out," asked Charlie. "Well, I don't think I would have been scared," said DJ. But I would have been aggravated and pissed off, that's for sure"!

Fortunately, they were able to charge Gage and Charlie's phones. "By the way," said Logan, talking to Gage and Charlie, "what were you guys thinking about going down that hallway without a charged phone"??

Neither Gage or Charlie said anything. What could they say..they wished they hadn't done it either.

"Hey guys…. what if the noises we heard were actually Max's gang hiding from us," said Gage. All of the boys stopped eating…stopped in their tracks and thought about it.

"Hey, what about starting a fire," said Logan. DJ thought about it, then shined his light up the fireplace. Amazingly, it looked clear! "I can't think why we shouldn't," said DJ. "Let's go find some firewood. We gotta watch out for grizzlies, so let's go out and stay fairly close together."

"Actually, gotta look out for everything," said Gage. "And look for wood that's dry, if possible. I wonder if those guys had firewood on the side of the house"? That made a lot of sense to the boys.

Logan went to the far side of the house with a covering, that looked as if there was gonna be wood, it would be here. He came around the corner, and heard a rustling from the far side, followed by a sound he had heard before…the growl of a mountain lion. 'GRRRRRRRRRRRRR" …..'GGGRRRRRRRRRRRRR'

Logan stood in his tracks for a second, then backed away slowly. He had his phone so he shined his light and could see the mountain lion rise. "HEY…. EASSSSYYY," said Logan. DJ heard Logan, so he walked over…calmly, but quickly.

"DJ you have your gun," asked Logan. "Always," said DJ, as he pulled out his pistol. He wasn't going to shoot what he thought was a momma mountain lion, but he needed to be ready!

"If figure she's got babies over there," said DJ. "We ain't getting wood from over there"! Slowly, they backed away, and they left each other alone. "I figure there's a lot of things out here that can hurt us," said Logan. "It's time for me to have a gun, DJ," said Logan.

"I agree," said DJ. "Plus, I think it's time for you to have a bigger role in the department. Let's talk about it with Sheriff and your dad when we return"!

They found some wood without any further problems and got ready for some sleep. The fireplace put out some pretty good heat! "Hey guys we still haven't checked out mansions 4 & 6," said DJ. "Before we take off, we need to hide the goods here, and then go over and make sure houses 1,2, 4 & 6, we can check them off."

The boys nodded yes, and within minutes, all of them were asleep. They almost expected some kind of crazy noise in the house. This was the first time they had slept in one of the mansions, and if Max's crew could do it, so could they!

About 4 in the morning, DJ got up to take a pee. He went to the back door, quietly opened it, and then went back in. There were at least four ways to come into the house, and at least two stairways. After all, this house was probably 8,000-10,000 sq feet!

As he was walking back in, he heard some creaking on the floors upstairs. He walked in to where the boys were sleeping, stood still, and listened. He didn't hear any talking, just noises, as if someone was walking upstairs. He naturally wondered if it were Max's gang up there, and if he had someone with him that had a gun, he'd go up there. But no way was he going to take that chance, for himself or the boys!

The boys woke up about 7 am. They all said they heard some kind of noises, from a faint scream, to sounding like someone was walking upstairs. "Yeah that's what I heard too," said DJ. "Anyways, before we get over to #5 & 6 Mansion, let's get the goods in a hiding place, for now."

"Hey, DJ, Gage, and I will go up and start bringing down rifles and pistols," said Logan. "But maybe before we do that, we'll take pictures. I'm sure that's why they lined up all their stuff, so they could get it sold ahead of time! And it will help us eventually get it catalogued."

Gage talked non-stop to his brother about what happened when he and Charlie got lost. They got up to the closet with the hidden door, opened I to start taking pictures, and…. the room was empty!!

"Okay, wait," said Logan. "Are there two of these stupid hidden rooms??" Given the size of #5 Mansion, it would totally make sense! DJ reckoned that this house was easily 15,000 square feet. They had a lot of rooms they never got to on this trip!

Gage and Logan just stood there thinking about it for a second. "DJ…CHARLIE…GET UP HERE," yelled Gage.

DJ and Charlie flew up the stairs… "See for yourself," said Gage. Both DJ and Charlie walked in. They couldn't believe what they were looking at. "There is just no way," said DJ. "Hey Charlie, do you see the Can-Am out there??"

They all went to the window, studying intensely in the area where they saw it last night. "It's gone," yelled Charlie. "OMG, they came here in the middle of the night! But HOW…HOW did they know to come last night? Or were they here the whole time we have been here"??

All four ran down the stairs from the 3rd floor, jumping two or three stairs at a time. They ran out the back door where they went last night and ran down the trail. "Yep…it's gone," said DJ. "Sheriff is NOT going to be happy, will be my guess"!

"Any chance they are still here?" Asked Charlie. "No, I don't think so," said DJ.

"I'm soooo glad we brought the bikes inside the house," said Logan. "But let's get back in, let's make sure everything is still in place, and get our work done." All the boys were pretty dejected, knowing that they got ripped off a second time and got outplayed by these criminals.

But no one felt as bad as DJ did. He radioed to the Sheriff and told him the bad news. The Sheriff actually consoled DJ. No way was it DJ's fault, and he agreed…it was time for either Logan to play a bigger role in the department, or have another deputy travel with him up the hill.

They finished the work in Mansions number 5 & 6 in about another hour. They buttoned everything up and made it down the mountain in about two hours. Dj and the boys, including Travis, Bobby, and of course Chloe, met up for dinner later at the diner, and told their stories of the last two days.

The Sheriff, DJ, Logan, and Jacob went off to the side for a bit to talk about Logan having a gun. "Look, not yet," said Sheriff. "Legally, you can't be a deputy." Logan was disappointed, but he knew the answer would probably be no.

"BUT…we can talk about you being a consultant," said Sheriff. Logan couldn't help but smile by now. Chloe didn't care if it was supposed to be a private conversation; she took her chances and sat next to Logan.

"Your dad and I think it's a good idea for you to have a pistol mainly for wildlife, to protect yourself and your group. What do you think…start as a paid consultant for the Sheriff department?" Logan looked over at his dad, who was smiling too. "Logan, you still have to start your college classes next semester," said Jacob. "But…what an incredible opportunity"!

Logan could only say two things. "Absolutely, I'm all in…and let's eat"!!

Mansion Number 1, by far the most eery of the houses! We believe we heard noises from inside. Maybe next time during the day we will go inside?!

Mansion No. 2 before the storm hit. Very eery house, beautiful inside!

CHAPTER 13

Charlie

The Moto Boys were together in one section of the hospital lobby. While, parents were in the other corner, with the Sheriff, DC, and DJ. No one was saying much, and they were stunned with what had just happened. Pastor Dave had just gotten to the hospital, and was making his way to the parents' group.

The owner of the diner, Jim, had just shown up with food, but no one was interested in eating. One thing about the town of Clear Springs, they came together when needed.

14 hours earlier, at around 6:30 pm, Wednesday night. Charlie's parents called Jacob Dalton, to see if Charlie was at their house. Charlie's parents were on the strict side, always knowing where their kids were, from school activities, the riding with the boys.

"Charlie is not here," said Jacob, "but I and the boys will go look for him now, I am sure he is close by here!"

Normally they finished riding right around 5:15-5:30 pm, when they rode during the week. They would ride all night if it didn't get dark and it was dinner time!

Jacob yelled out to the boys, told Logan to take his mom's car with Gage, while he took his pick-up truck the other way. Logan grabbed

Chloe from next door to go with them and look.

Pretty soon everyone from the Moto Boys to neighbors, were out looking for Charlie. It was almost impossible that he could get lost on the way home. Of course, people always worried about grizzlies and mountain lions in this town!

"Logan I'm scared," said Chloe from the back seat. "No way, that kid is just fine', said Gage. But everyone was worried. It was dark, with no sign of any moon out tonight!

Everyone in sight was crawling in their cars. Bright spotlights were scouring the brush. You could see the outline of the lights from the Sheriff's truck and the Fire Truck in the distance.

"CHARLIE...CHARLIE" ...everyone was yelling from their cars. "Sheriff says to come to Sunset and Meadow View...NOW"! DJ was calling Logan over his cell phone. Logan hit the gas pedal all the way,

burning rubber as he took off. "Put your seat belts on guys," said Logan. DJ didn't say anything other than "get to Sunset and Meadow View."

Sheriff was already on scene, with the Fire Captain's truck coming fast from the other direction, with lights and siren! DJ had jumped already into the ditch. Gage didn't even wait for the car to stop. Before Logan could take off with his brother, the Sheriff called out to him…

"Logan, pull your car sideways, and block the road," said Sheriff.

Logan jumped out of his mom's SUV after pulling it sideways. Jacob, Logan and Gage's dad were now on scene. "Apparently Cindy, our neighbor, saw two wolves near something or someone in the ditch…and she thought it could be Charlie," said Jacob.

Both Gage and Logan jumped into the ditch, alongside DJ. The water was running slow, probably 12 inches deep, with mud on all sides of the ditch. The body was laying sideways, his left hand was just touching the water in the ditch. There was blood was by his head.

It was definitely Charlie….and he was unconscious!!

DJ, a former Medic and Ranger in the Army, was leaning over Charlie, feeling for a pulse and breathing. "Charlie, we're here, buddy," said both Logan and Gage, in very loud, scared, and almost out of breath voices!

"He's breathing, and he has a very faint pulse," said DJ!! Charlie did not move or make any motion. DJ was smart enough to not move him, except gently pulling his fingers out of the water.

"Hey, Sanjay, we have Charlie," said the Sheriff, calling Charlie's dad.

"He's alive, we just got here, and I'm calling for an air lift. Sanjay…he's badly hurt! We're at the corner of Sunset and Meadow View, I am sending Deputy Colton to come and get you guys!"

DC didn't wait for any further instructions. He jumped into the truck to go and get Charlie's parents. Jacob and Margie Dalton also arrived on scene. Chloe ran over to Margie in tears; they both needed someone to hug!

"This is Sheriff Walden requesting immediate Airlift, this is a critical situation…I repeat, critical situation," said Sheriff.

"We're located at the corner of Sunset and Meadow View in Clear Springs. We'll flood the area with light, and we have plenty of room to land on the street"!

"I repeat, this is Sheriff Walden, requesting a critical air-lift…NOW!!

Jacob went and moved his truck back and blocked one end of the road, with Logan blocking the other end; now there was plenty of room for the helicopter to land.

Deputy Colton pulled up 30 seconds later with Charlie's parents. Charlie's dad, Sanjay, jumped out and went right over to the ditch. Margie went over to Charlie's mom, Maya, and put her arm around her, telling her softly that she did not know much yet, but he had a pulse and was breathing. Charlie's younger sister, Anna, stuck close to her mom.

"Logan, any idea yet how this happened," asked Charlie's mom, tears running down her cheeks. "Who the hell would want to hurt such a sweet boy." This made Chloe break down crying; Margie put her arm around both of them.

"No idea yet," said Logan, very quietly. His eyes on DJ and Charlie, and DJ was tending to the bleeding on Charlie's forehead. You could hear the helicopter coming over the mountain, with the noise from the chopper getting stronger and stronger. 20 seconds later, you could see the chopper in the air. By now, both Travis and Bobby were on scene with their parents.

"Okay, I want everyone shining and waving flashlights for the bird," yelled out the Sheriff! "Let's start making way for its landing"! The helicopter passed over them, and started to circle down. Within 30 seconds, it was directly overhead, making way to land.

Everyone moved back about 20 yards, and only DJ, Logan, and Gage were leaning over Charlie to protect him from the wind of the helicopter. The wind from the helicopter blade was strong, blowing wind everywhere, including a few caps that people didn't hold tight. It seemed like forever for the chopper to touch down. Before the air ambulance even landed, two paramedics jumped into the ditch without hitting the water or Charlie.

"I'm Deputy DJ, this is Charlie," said DJ. We don't know how long he's been here, we're guessing about 30-45 minutes, nor do we know exactly what happened here"! One of the people that came out of the Air Ambulance was an Emergency doctor that came with them; he went right to work on Charlie's vitals, and started an IV immediately. They were amazingly calm and precise in their work!

DJ also was amazingly calm in this situation, but we also know how he felt about the Moto Boys. They were family to him!

The paramedics put a collar around Charlie, rolled his body up, placed him on the stretcher. By now, everyone had made room for the paramedics to do their work. As they were placing him into the helicopter, they wrapped Charlie in thermal blankets. The paramedics continued to take Charlie's vitals, while at the same time, radioing to the hospital…getting ready for lift-off.

"We have room for one parent," said the Paramedic, as the helicopter's engine got louder. Sanjay and Maya looked at each other, and they decided Charlie's dad would ride in the helicopter.

The helicopter lifted off, and within seconds, it was over the mountain, with one of the Moto Boys in critical condition. No one said a word, everyone was in shock, you could hear most everyone there trying to sniff back their tears. "I am heading to the hospital now if anyone needs a ride. Travis and Bobby looked at their parents, they nodded approvingly as to say "yes, go."

"Maya, come with us," said Margie. "Logan, you drive your brother to the hospital," said Jacob. "Chloe, you can go with Logan and Gage.

Logan and Gage went up to DJ to start to ask a few questions about what had just happened. DJ's demeanor and attitude had changed from when he first was at the hospital, from standing, to now pacing back and forth. Now he looked pissed!

About 1.5 hours after Charlie had arrived at the hospital, the doctor came out, still dressed in his scrubs. He waited for everyone to gather around. Charlies parents and daughter came up to the front of the group. "Okay, so, the good news, Charlie is stable for the time," said Dr. Ravidan, one of the area's top neurosurgeons. "But, he's lost a tremendous amount of blood. I'll start by saying thank god it wasn't any later you found him." Everyone that could reach Charlie's parents gently placed hands on their shoulders.

"We were able to drain blood from his brain by doing a craniotomy, first and foremost. We saw immediate improvement in his vitals," Doc continued. "He has a lot of injuries!! A broken jaw, and a right lower leg fracture."

You could hear several parents crying as the doctor was telling them about Charlie's injuries. "We'll do surgery for the jaw fracture most likely around noon tomorrow," said Dr. Ravidan. "Followed by his lower leg surgery, probably over the weekend."

"But listen, again I am repeating myself, thank god you guys found Charlie when you did," said Dr. Ravidan. "Another hour and I believe Charlie would not have made it!" By this point there was not a dry eye in the room, including Sheriff; he was a very stoic person, that never showed his emotions. But tonight, everyone showed their emotions!

"We don't know how well Charlie will come out of this," said the Doc. But if you believe in miracles, PLUS our amazing surgical team, this is a good time for you to pray for Charlie and our team"!!

"I think this might be a good time to go home and get rest, you won't be able to see Charlie tonight, but in case you're still here, I'll come and check on you guys in a bit," said Dr. Ravidan.

"I have another patient to tend to right now."

Everyone thanked the Doctor. Before he left, Sheriff spoke up, and even though the doctor just said no visitors, he asked anyways. "Not yet," said the doc, as he was walking away, back thru the double doors.

No one was leaving. Without anyone saying a word, everyone walked up to Sanjay and Maya, and placed hands on their shoulders. DJ led them all in a short but powerful prayer. "Thank you all," said Charlie's dad. "This means a lot, almost the world to us, and Charlie for sure!"

The boys walked over to DJ, Sheriff and Deputy Colton. "Look I know it's early, but any ideas Sheriff," asked Logan. Everyone could get a sense of what they were talking about, so they all started trying to listen to what Sheriff was going to say. "You're right, too early to say much," said Sheriff. "Here's what we do know. First, Charlie's bike is gone. I could care less about the bike, but it does tell me that perhaps, at least my first thought, is this is a robbery for a bike that went bad."

Everyone was quiet, waiting for the Sheriff to say something. "I agree with Sheriff, this looks like a robbery gone bad," and we aren't going to get many answers until we get to talk to Charlie," said DJ. "I'm not going to get ahead of myself, but I want to make this right for Charlie…that's all I'm going to say"!!

Everyone knew that DJ wanted to exact revenge on whoever did this to Charlie, but now was not the time to get angry or show negative emotions. Charlie's parents needed positive support right now!"

The Sheriff from Kalispell showed up to the hospital, walking fast over to Sheriff Don and the group. "Hey guys, I just heard about 20 minutes ago," said Sheriff Joe. "Whatever you guys need, support wise," all you have to do is ask. Look, I know this is not the time to talk about anything else, but we know that at least one group is up riding and camping at Silver Mines and the Mansions, raising hell."

Sheriff Don spoke up. "Did you get a Deputy up there to see it," asked Sheriff.

"The problem is, we have too many entrances to get into both areas!" The Sheriff brought his voice down. He really didn't want to talk about anything but Charlie right now, but, unfortunately, they had to address this new problem.

"There's at least 5 trails we know of to get up to the ghost towns," said DJ. "We know we can control Eagles Crossing. Sheriff Joe, can you guys tear down that little bridge we built last week up at Silver Mines Estates, and block that off"? Sheriff Joe didn't say a word, he just nodded yes.

"Sheriff, I can put together a plan to get those guys off the mountain, I'll take Logan and Gage with me tomorrow, we can leave about 11 am. We'll plan on sleeping up there one night," said DJ. That meant a couple more days of missed school, but honestly, there wasn't a choice. If people rode up there all the time, those areas would get completely destroyed!

Bobby and Travis had just gotten their new bikes last week, but only rode them for about one hour. The Deputy for Sheriff Joe also rode his bike one time with the Moto Boys. He was a lot like DJ; fit, very athletic, and was a great fit with the boys. He also had prior experience riding. He also was super impressed with how well the boys rode, and couldn't believe how fast Gage and Logan rode!

"Sheriff Joe, can you spare Deputy Mitch to go with us tomorrow," asked DJ. Sheriff Joe looked over at him with a smile, "Are you kidding, I guarantee he's ready to ride! Plus, he rode on his own the last two days…he won't embarrass you or himself!"

Bobby went over to ask his parents if they could go, provided of course, that they were included in this trip. Travis was just not ready, and that was fine with the Sheriff and DJ.

Everyone gave their hugs and goodbyes for now. Charlie's parents and his sister were of course, going to stay at the hospital, looking for any updates they could provide everyone.

It was a scary and tragic day, and Charlie wasn't out of the woods, but everyone could go to bed knowing they'd found Charlie, and, he was going to live!

CHAPTER 14

Chaos

Everyone arrived on time the next morning at Eagles Crossing, ready to ride by 11:10 am.

"Hey guys, update on Charlie," said DJ. "He woke up this morning and is in surgery now. They're putting two plates in his lower jaw – it was broken in two places."

Gage and Logan exchanged grim looks, both shaken by the thought of how hard Charlie must've been hit. Two breaks? That was brutal. And the wolves sniffing around the night before—if one had gone for Charlie's throat, it would have been over!

The directive was clear and focused. Get the idiots out of both Silver Mines and the Silver Mines Mansions, before they get hurt, trash the area or start a fire. What really worried Sheriff about these guys was the potential for the word to spread – if these guys kept partying like this, the mountain, the mansions, and the wilderness could be destroyed. having the time of their lives, and the word spreads; pretty soon Silver Mines would also get destroyed,

Deputy Mitch— "DM" to the crew—was riding with the Moto Boys for the first time. He didn't say much, naturally, and everyone was sure he was at least a little nervous. His first trip with the Moto Boys and DJ, and there was a lot to remember. "Hey DM, I will lead us into #1 and #2, you follow Gage, Logan goes behind you.

Mitch watched Gage shoot over the top of EC, with Logan tight on his heels. Bobby, on his brand-new Yamaha WR250F, wasn't far behind, his bike was incredibly fast.

And down the hill went DM; when he was choosing what bike, he was going to get, Mitch also decided on the WR 250F. It was now the bike Gage and Logan recommended.

Mitch did a small wheelie through the water, was in the right gear at the base of the hill. Suddenly, halfway up, DM tapped by mistake his gearshift, and it popped out of gear. Fortunately, DM did a good job of getting the bike sideways on the hill, pointed it back down, and started back up. This time he flew up the hill with no problems.

DJ kept pace with Gage over the other side. Before heading into Forest #1, they waved goodbye to Jacob and Chloe's dad, who drove their trucks back to Jacob's house instead of leaving them at Eagles Crossing.

It was a picture-perfect day, but like always, when you enter into these deep forests, it looks like nighttime inside of 30 seconds. They were about two minutes in, and DJ motioned for them to stop.

"Just checking in," DJ said. "Also, Mitch—I want you to hear the silence in here."

Mitch scanned the dense shadows, speaking in a hushed tone. "This is crazy..." said Mitch, in a quiet, muffled voice, as if he didn't want to wake up any animals inside the forest.

DJ and Logan had told him about the "Screamers" they had met, and at first, Mitch thought they were just messing with him. Mitch rode well on the single tracks through #1, and made it thru the water with no problem. As they were getting out of upper side of #1, the meadows were stunning, so green and beautiful. Until DJ saw the damage!

DJ saw the other tracks all over the meadow, and, he and the boys could tell that these guys had torn up the meadow with their bikes. NOW, DJ was pissed!! The meadows were super important for wild animals to protect their babies, and no telling just how many animals were now exposed or killed as a result of these stupid acts!

"I swear I'll lock these guys up for this," said DJ. "Just no telling what else they screwed up at Silver Mines"! DJ, Mitch, and the boys took as many pics as they could before heading into #2.

The ride into #2 was uneventful, and before they headed up the hill into Silver Mines, they stopped to listen for bikes.

"Hey Sheriff, DJ here, can you hear us," asked DJ. He radioed one more time, and before he got the question out, Sheriff answered back.

"Hey, DJ, "said Sheriff. "You at Silver Mines?"

"We're about to go into Silver Mines, we don't hear any," said DJ as he cut what he was saying short. "Wait, we hear something……guys, let's get out of sight," said DJ, in a short-abbreviated voice! They all hit the start button and moved their bikes under the closest pine tree.

Up at the top of the hill, these guys had created a race track, including the back of Silver Mines. One look and you could tell that these guys were good riders; in fact, they were very good riders, perhaps at the level of Gage!

By now, all the boys were pressed close together. No one said a word, it was clear DJ was trying to figure out a plan. "DJ, this is the perfect time to hit the hill, said Logan. While they're racing…let's start running laps with these guys, and we suddenly hit stop. They won't know what hit them"!! "LET'S GO," said DJ!

They all fired up the bikes, when suddenly Mitch waved his arms, "WAIT"! Everyone turned their bikes off again. "Guys, this is not a great plan," said Mitch.

I think I have a better plan! And you guys already did it once!

After Mitch explained it, everyone knew this plan was solid. "I knew there was a reason you joined us," said Logan. "Okay, guys, let's get some rest, and then when it's dark, we enter the back side of the town, we go to sleep, and in the am, we sneak up on them, and we basically capture them for the ride home tomorrow."

At 5:30 p.m., the engines went silent. The bikers were likely in the old Silver Mines Hotel for dinner. But DJ cursed under his breath when he heard a dog barking—a big one, likely brought along in a Can-Am.

"Okay we aren't sleeping next to them, that's out," said DJ. "Tonight, we sleep in the schoolhouse, which is actually safer for us. After all, we aren't terribly interested in what they have to say."

"We just have to get up early enough to surprise the crap out of them before they start riding," said Mitch. "It's getting cold, I say we get up out of this cold air," said Bobby.

"I agree, let's hide the bikes," said DJ. "Let's climb the mountain, and instead of going left behind the town, we go right, then, sneak into the back of the schoolhouse."

By 6:10, they were all up the hill, and headed to the back of the church. "My guess is they won't let their dog take off if they hear us, because they would be worried he would be chasing a wolf or a mountain lion," said Gage. "Smart Gage…very smart," said Mitch.

Before making the cross over to the church, they looked down the street, and they had set up a big bonfire in the middle of the main road of Silver Mines, with a small bbq set up. They had loud music playing…VERY loud music, which really helped the boys…they just had to be sure they weren't seen!

They got settled into the schoolhouse. "Are you kidding me," said DJ. You could tell he was upset, as he was when he saw the tracks in the meadows. There were tire tracks inside the schoolhouse, and you could tell they had beat up some of the wood structures inside.

"These guys are complete morons," said Logan. "Sheriff come in, can you hear me," said Mitch from the satellite phone. "I can hear you DJ," what is happening," said the Sheriff. I'm here at the diner with Jacob, let us walk outside so we can talk."

"Okay we're here," said Sheriff. "First let me give you some news about Charlie. He's alert, had his jaw wired shut, surgery was successful. Tomorrow am, he has his surgery for his arm," said Sheriff. "But get this…he was able to tell us, with a marker board, that they had stolen his bike, forced him into their truck, and tried putting a bag over his head."

The Sheriff stopped for a minute to make sure no one around was listening.

"Okay, this part is hard to hear," said Sheriff. "When they went to put a bag over Charlie's head, Charlie bit down on the guy's finger…Charlie said he bit the crap out of him. That is the GOOD part"!

"But, then they beat the hell out of poor Charlie, slugging him while he was still in the truck…and while their truck was moving, they kicked him out of the truck, and he fell into the ditch! He doesn't remember anything after that point"!

All of the boys, DJ, Mitch…they were stone cold silent, just listening. "You guys still there," said Sheriff.

"Yeah we are just taking it all in," said DJ. Hearing this made the task at hand tougher, because they all wanted to be looking for the jerks that did this to Charlie!

"Hey Sheriff, have you done a search for anyone in the area that was treated for a bite," said DJ. "Two steps ahead," said Sheriff.

"Looking for anyone that was treated for a bite, and for anyone that got antibiotics and or tetanus shot for a bite…we searched throughout the state!"

"And, we just might have good news," said Jac0b. "We have a suspect we're visiting when DJ and Mitch get back"!

It was such amazing news that Charlie was making good progress, but to hear that he was kidnapped, beaten to a pulp, and left for dead was hard to hear! They all told the Sheriff and Jacob to give Charlie their best!

It didn't make sense to Logan that they weren't going after him yet, and were waiting for DJ and Mitch to get back, but they knew the Sheriff must have his reasons.

DJ turned the attention back to talking about Silver Mines, and told Sheriff and Jacob their plan. He told them they planned on being back around 1 pm, god willing and the creek don't rise. That saying actually had some meaning in the mountains of Montana!

The boys went back to watching these guys at the end of the road. While their music was going, Logan had an idea. "I think you and Mitch should go see just how many guys they have while they are playing this loud of music." DJ looked at Mitch to get his thoughts. "I think it's a good idea," said Mitch.

"I see one woman, a big dog, and I think four guys."

When a few of these guys fired up a couple of the bikes, Mitch and DJ went out the backdoor of the schoolhouse. There was a half-moon coming out, and being this high up on the mountain, it was pretty bright. Bright enough for these guys to have drag races up the main street of Silver Mines.

These guys drag racing up and down the street made it easier for DJ and Mitch to make it up the backside of the street. One pair went, one racing his Honda 450F, the other a Yamaha WR 250F. "I have to admit, it looks super fun," said Gage.

The next guys to go, and three guys lined up…so now they knew there were at least 5 bikes. Two of the guys had CRF 450 RL, and the other was a Yamaha WR 250F. One of the 450's whipped the other two guys, and they rode all the way to the beginning of the church.

As they turned around, Gage noticed the Yamaha had a sticker on the back fender. The only other time they had seen that sticker, and in the place, it was on the fender…was Charlie's bike!

Could it possibly be Charlie's??

These guys continued riding wheelies for a bit. Like idiots, they started riding on the wooden sidewalks in the town, which definitely was going to chew up the walkways. The rode up to the church, and it was clear they were going to go inside the church.

"I cannot believe what these idiots are doing," said Logan. All of the boys were in shock. "What they're doing is completely insane," Gage whispered. "Racing inside the church! Their tires had to be tearing up the floor."

"We have to be ready for these guys to come back inside the schoolhouse," said Logan. "If we see them coming this way, we go out the back door!"

Finally, they left the church, and turned off the bikes. They were still laughing and drinking beer when they sat down around their fire.

"Man, I would like to have a fire like those guys," DJ muttered. "Did you guys see that decal on the back fender of the Yamaha?" asked Gage. Mitch and DJ shook their heads.

Gage explained what he saw, and DJ frowned. "If that was Charlie's bike, it's unlikely someone's riding it—he bit one of them hard enough to send him to the hospital."

"Well…maybe he gave the bike to someone else in his gang to ride," said Gage. "But hey…can we get the ID numbers for Charlie's bike from his parents before tomorrow am," asked Logan.

"Absolutely, great idea," said DJ, as he dialed the satellite phone to call the Sheriff to get the ID number!

The next morning, everyone was ready at 7:30 am. "Okay, we go around the back side, said DJ "The dog will be inside, and I doubt they will let their dog out this early. It's a big German Shepard, so we aren't just walking in the door. They could see their bikes, leaning against the walls on the front side of the Hotel where they were staying.

They were stealth-mode walking on the back side. "Okay, all of us are close together, but just in case they decide to try and shoot us, Mitch and I will have our P-320's out and ready…just in case."

As they crept toward the front, the peace shattered—the dog started barking. Loud.

"Knock knock," said DJ, at the same time he knocked. Logan, Gage and Bobby were peering out one side of the front window, with Mitch on the other side of the glass.

"Knock knock," again said DJ at the same time he knocked. He would have walked in if there wasn't a German shepherd inside!

"What the f…..," said one of the riders inside.

"HANG ON…I'm coming…hey, hold Stormy back"! He was clearly pissed. He opened the door, still half asleep. Before he said anything, he peered out the door, looking at the five guys at his doorstep.

"Good morning, I'm DJ. And you are," asked DJ, as he extended his hand to shake.

"Who the hell are you guys, and why are you waking us up," said the still un-named guy.

"My name is DJ, also known as Deputy John, and this is Deputy Mitch," said DJ.

"You guys known damn well you aren't supposed to be here. We had signs everywhere to NOT ride up the mountain."

"The Deputy asked you…what is your name?" asked Mitch, this time a little stronger.

"Steve. And we haven't done anything wrong."

By then, Steve's other guys were at the front door. DJ pressed himself inside.

"I am coming in, please make sure you hold on to your dog," said DJ.

"Hey, I didn't say you could come in where we're sleeping," said Steve.

"Well, Steve, I didn't have to ask you if we could come in," said DJ. Steve's eyes widened. "What?! For what?"

"What do you mean under arrest," said Steve, now in a very pissed off mood.

"We didn't do ANYTHING wrong!" DJ looked back at Mitch and the boys. Before DJ answered, Logan whispered in his ear about the Yamaha one of them was riding.

"Oh really," said DJ. You're trespassing. That's one. You trashed a protected meadow. That's two. You rode dirt bikes inside a church and broke a pew, not to mention, rode inside the schoolhouse… That's three. And four…" DJ glanced back at the others. Logan whispered something in his ear.

No one answered at first, as if they didn't hear DJ.

"Did you hear the Deputy?" asked Mitch, in a louder voice.

"WHO IS RIDING THE YAMAHA…you know, the blue bike out there?"

"That belongs to Russell," said Steve, turning around to point to the guy named Russel.

"Where is that guy?" Whoever Russel was, he wasn't inside. "Maybe he went outside to take a piss," said Steve.

"Deputy, he ain't part of our group," said one of the other guys that hadn't introduced himself as of yet. DJ started to ask the obvious question, when they heard a bike start up outside and take off.

"Oh shit, he's taking off," said Gage. They wanted to chase after him in the worst way, but they had not brought the bikes back up to Silver Mines yet.

"Tell you what," said DJ. Mitch and I will stay here with these guys, you guys get your bikes, then you can double back and get our bikes."

"Crap I want to chase this dude," Gage clenched his fists.

"Well, knowing what we know, would you want to go down this mountain by yourself," said Logan. Both Gage and Logan just shook their heads no way! TOOO many things to go wrong! The boys jogged down the hill to get their bikes, and within 20 minutes, they had all 5 bikes up in front of the saloon.

DJ kept an eye on their German shepherd. This whole situation was a mess at best, but if they stayed organized, they would have these guys in handcuffs at the end of the day.

DJ called Sheriff on the satellite phone and kept him appraised of the situation. "Sheriff, one the guys took off on us, it's my fault," said DJ.

"I'm not sure how it's your fault, DJ," said Sheriff. But, overall, if you guys can get down the hill in one piece, and we take these away in cuffs, it's a great day!"

"Okay, guys, needless to say, you have a lot to answer for when we get back to town," said DJ.

"You have NO idea how dangerous this ride down the mountain can be, so I'll lead us out, then Gage, then you guys, and then Mitch, then Logan."

Then he turned to the other two riders. "You'll take the Can-Am down the way you came—with the dog."

Mitch added, "And you are putting goggles on that dog, right?" The two that were taking the Can Am looked at each other, and asked "why would we put goggles on a dog"?

Mitch rolled his eyes. "Oh my God." His voice was full of frustration. Mitch was a diehard animal lover—with two dogs of his own.

"You will crush his eyes," so put some damn goggles on her, or, I will add animal cruelty to the mix!!"

"Before we take off," said DJ. "You could really help your situation with the right information. Did you know that the Yamaha was stolen"? Steve looked around at his group before answering.

"We had no idea who he was," said Steve. "He and his buddies saw our truck in town at the bar outside of town, and we got to talking, we told him we were going riding up here. One of the guys, Russell, asked if he could go with us, that is all I know."

"Was there someone in their group who looked like he got hurt," said Logan. "Is he a deputy too," asked Steve.

"No, but I will ask you the exact same question," said Mitch.

"Actually, they asked if they had a drug store in town, and if there was an urgent care in town," said one of the other guys. "My name is Jeff."

DJ put his kickstand back down. They were all anxious to get going, but DJ wanted more information…a LOT more information.

"Okay, Jeff, so what did you say next," asked DJ.

"We told him we're not from here," said Jeff. We're from Billings. We knew of Urgent care centers in Billings…because one of us is always getting hurt. We didn't ask any other questions, and they didn't say anything more about it."

"Sheriff, come in," said DJ. "Hey, DJ, I'm here, said the Sheriff. "Well, it was Charlie's bike, and while we were starting to talk to these guys, the guy riding the Yamaha sneaked out the back of the hotel, and rode off. Our bikes were still down the hill. I'm sorry Sheriff."

"So, he is riding back down by himself?" asked the Sheriff.

"I'm more worried about him getting real hurt than I am him getting away. You guys need to get down the hill to see if you find him or catch up to him. We'll be on the lookout for him AND the Can Am!"

"One last question," said DJ.

"Well before I ask the question, we're going to use some of your gas, you guys make sure your bikes are gassed up. How good a rider was this Russell guy, and how good of riders are you guys?"

"He was okay," said Jeff. "Not as good as us…and I would imagine we are much better riders than you guys." DJ looked at the boys and Mitch to get their reaction to this information, and no one said a word. Gage just had a wry smile under his helmet. "Well, if you are better riders than these two, then you are amazing riders," said Mitch, pointing at Logan and Gage.

As they started down the hill, the boys could tell these guys were very good riders. It would be stupid to try and get away with anything, with the Sheriff waiting for them at the bottom of the hill. DJ stopped at the first meadow before entering #2, raising his hand to have everyone turn their bikes off.

"Well, I don't need to take more pictures of this screwed up meadow, do we gentleman," said DJ.

"You have any idea how many wild animals you displaced, killed…by riding in this grass?"

"Well, I know you don't have to believe us," said Steve.

"But it was Russell who started it, we were in a hurry to get up the hill."

"So, are you saying you didn't ride in it," asked Mitch. "I think we're done answering questions," said Steve.

"Let's just get down the hill." Considering how many were now riding in this group, they made great time getting through #2. They were good riders, but Logan could tell they weren't close to Gage and his level of riding.

These guys made the same tracks thru the meadow between #1 and #2, and there was no sense in stopping to point it out. But DJ did point to it as he was riding, just to drive the point home. It truly was disgusting what this Russell guy had done. DJ assumed at least one or more of these guys rode in the meadows, since they didn't deny it.

About 10 am, they were about one third thru #1, when they heard it. The boys and DJ had heard it so many times it didn't scare them this time. Mitch was warned, so he was expecting it. But these guys going down…well, it was another story!

"BRAOOOOROOORAAAR"… …"BRAOOOOROOORAAAR"

Everyone stopped. "What the hell is that noise?" screamed Jeff. They had now stopped turned off their bikes. "Hey guys, what the hell is that noise," asked Jeff again, this time sounding a little more scared.

"What noise," said Gage. "I think it's just wolves." Gage has a smile on his face, knowing it was scaring the crap out of these guys.

DJ got off his bike, as he looked a little in front of him, and down the hill, off the trail, was Charlie's Yamaha. Which meant Russell was down the hill at the bottom of the ravine. "If only that was the one that hurt Charlie," said DJ to Logan, as Logan had caught up to DJ, looking at Charlie's Yamaha.

By now everyone was off of their bikes, and the other two guys with Steve and Jeff were looking everywhere for where this super loud noise was coming.

"HELP...HELP." The yelling was coming from the bottom of the ravine, where Russell had fallen. This was similar to the area that caught both Bobby and Travis, although they hadn't fallen as far as this Russell dude did; he was way down at the bottom!!

"Hey...your name is Russell, right? Are you okay?" yelled DJ, down to Russell. "Yeah, I'm okay," said Russell, sounding a little dejected. Surely, he had hoped for a clear getaway, and now that was out the window.

"Okay, we're tying two ropes together," said Mitch.

Both DJ and Mitch jumped into action, working together to get him back up. They created a plan to get his bike back up first, because it was in the path to pull Russell up.

"BRAOOOOROOORAAAR"... ..."BRAOOOOROOORAAAR"

Gage and Logan looked to their left, and they saw the Screamers, not completely hiding, but not, however, totally in view for everyone to see. Logan looked over to Bobby, to quietly show him where to look. He didn't, however, want to point it out to Steve's group...he wanted them to be freaked out!

"Seriously guys, what the hell is that noise," asked Jeff, sounding completely freaked out. Everyone ignored these guys, at least for now, as they had a lot of work to get Russell up the hill. DJ had to yell, because this guy had fallen a long way down the mountain. "PLEASE help me up, this is pretty damn freaky down here"!!

DJ instantly said, making the most of that opportunity, "if we help you up the hill, will you answer our questions," but that could later create problems in court, and it was surely going to end up being heard in court.

"Okay, we're getting your bike out of the way, then pulling you up," yelled DJ. "Okay, all of you guys help us get his bike up, I am going down to tie the rope to his back rim," said Mitch. He was very fit, and very adept at getting down the hill, tie on the rope, and get back up the hill in like zero time!

Charlie's Yamaha was still in good shape, no worse for wear for sliding down the hill. It was going to take both ropes to reach him.

"Okay, tie it around your waist, and use your feet to help us bring you up. DJ also saw the Screamers, and he couldn't help but wonder, could they help, or would they make things worse?

"Hey, look, over behind the tree, what is that….is that like Big Foot," asked Steve. "Whatever that is…it looks like it could kill us. Dude, why don't you shoot at it"! DJ just smiled over at Logan and Gage. DJ acted like he didn't even hear Steve.

"First of all, it's Deputy to you, not dude," said DJ. "Only help we need is getting this guy out of the ravine, so get over here and help pull the rope!"

"These freaks are freaking us out," said Jeff. What really worried DJ, Mitch and the boys were these guys telling other about the Screamers, and eventually, creating bigger problems.

But the Screamers were not doing anything else to hurt these guys. It seemed as if they were making their "screams" to point out that someone was at the bottom of the ravine, in case they hadn't seen this guy.

And now that they were pulling Russell up, the Screamers weren't making any noise, and now weren't seen behind the tree.

Finally, they got Russell up to the top, and made sure he got a drink of water. "I'm guessing you won't try anything stupid will you now," said DJ. "No doubt you know you're riding a stolen bike, and I am guessing you have information for us, regarding your buddy with the finger bite."

"Lawyer, lawyer, lawyer," said Russell. "He was not my buddy, I met him for the first time. I know my rights…even in the middle of the damn forest"! DJ just looked over at Logan and Mitch, shaking his head.

"Ride careful, Russell," said Mitch. Russell didn't say a word as he got on his bike…Charlies bike!

The rest of the ride home was non-eventful, and both Sheriffs were waiting to take the whole gang to jail. Sheriff Joe's deputies were waiting for the Can Am on the other road to Silver Mines.

All of these guys took the "lawyer" route. Every one of them. But now, they had zero leverage!

For the first time ever, the small quiet towns of Clear Springs and Whispering Pines didn't feel safe. There were noise complaints almost every day, and even worse, theft was up in both towns. The surrounding counties also had record amounts of theft, stealing mostly guns and jewelry. The beloved diner seemed to always have someone being loud or causing problems!

But first things first…it was time to find the guy who almost killed Charlie!

CHAPTER 15

Catching a Snake

It felt like forever since the Moto Boys had all sat down for a meal at the diner. Sharing food, catching up, and hearing about Charlie's ankle surgery – which in typical surgeon speak, was "uneventful," which meant it went very well.

Logan hadn't had much opportunity lately to be with his girl, Chloe, so having her there made the night even better. She lit up when he invited her to join the guys.

It would be another three weeks before Charlie could talk, but he was able to use a marker board, and the boys would be able to see him tomorrow along with DJ. The guys they brought back from Silver Mines, "Steve's gang," were all being held in Kalispell.

Both Sheriffs were very strict about keeping this "Russell dude," from contacting anyone on the outside. They didn't want to risk tipping off his crew.

The Sheriff joined the boys as the dinner wrapped up, along with Logan and Gage's dad. Jacob was going to be a part of the plan– helping transport bikes deeper into the country at the drop off point.

"Hey guys, I haven't had a chance to thank you guys once again for a great job," said Sheriff.

"It's imperative we save Silver Mines. One day, we hope it'll be a ghost town people can safely visit," said Sheriff.

"Also, the Silver Mines Estates, or Mansions as you like to call them, need to be preserved too. I think most of you experienced them, yes"? Chloe looked at Logan and smiled, as if to say, "I remember those haunted mansions"!

"The cameras we put up, are working great," said Sheriff. "Every time you guys go up there, we'll bring more no trespassing signs, because we know they will tear them down. Plus, I want you guys to bring additional cameras, in case these idiots who go up there find the cameras!

The Sheriff moved into the middle of the guys, and brought his voice down. "Needless to say, this stays here," said the Sheriff.

"We investigated in all counties for anyone treated for a bite, and we found a doctor from an Urgent Care in Kalispell who treated a guy who matched what Charlie told us.

"And it matched the antibiotics purchased the same day," said Sheriff. "No surprise, he gave a fake address at the doctor, but Sheriff Joe and his deputies tracked down where we're pretty sure he's hiding out.

And it is way up on a mountain outside of Kalispell, with a gate, barbed wire, and at least two Rottweiler guard dogs"!

"And if we broke down the gate with our truck, and came right up his road, we know they will split out the back, and there are a million ways to hide up there. Eventually we will get this a-hole, but we want him now"! These are bad dudes"!!

"So, guys," said Mitch," I know this area like the back of my hand. I have hiked part of this, and it is way too far to hike all the way to their property. This is where we need your help"!

"In all seriousness," said DJ, "We have a map of the mountain trails in the area, and there's some nasty elevation changes, very narrow and rocky trails. Like Mitch says, we've never been on these trails. We expect this ride to be really difficult. So, we need Gage and Logan to show us how to navigate some of the areas!"

Gage and Logan looked at each other, and Gage was smiling. What a fantastic way to help the Sheriffs, plus hopefully get the guy that really hurt Charlie.

"You'll help us get about a quarter of the mile from their hideout," said Mitch. "From there, you guys have to stay there, we start walking to the back of their property and wait for us." Mitch looked around to make sure they understood the plan.

"Bobby and Travis, we have a huge favor to ask," asked Mitch.

"We want you, Gage and Logan to help train like in zero time, one of our other Deputies to ride, and because we don't have time to get another bike, will you loan him your bike"?

Bobby got a big smile over his face, that he could do a favor of that magnitude to get the guy who almost killed their friend.

"Absolutely…you bet," said both of them. Everyone was patting these guys on the back.

"Anything for Charlie," said Bobby.

"The bad news," said Sheriff, "you guys are gonna miss school." Everyone started laughing out loud. "Okay this one time," said Gage smiling.

"So, I'm sure you guys have thought about this already," said Travis. But, why not blow through their gate from the front, and avoid these crazy trails"? DJ grabbed a piece of paper and drew out a diagram of these guys property.

"We could do that, we've already scoped out the front," said DJ.

"Like we said, these guys have it not only gated, with barb wire around the top, with guard dogs. But the road up to the house is long…about a quarter mile…and that gives them plenty of time to get out the back, or go thru the woods to get to their neighbors!

One of the other two deputies, Robbie, spoke up. "I went to this property once before to arrest one of the guys living at this property," said Jeff.

"We were not successful. Like the Sheriff said, these are bad dudes living here! If they had just stolen Charlie's bike…chances are we would just let it go."

"But with attempted murder, and kidnapping," said the other Deputy, named Matt. That's worth a different attack plan!"

DJ was sending a text to all the moto boys. "Here is a list of all of the deputies involved in this plan," said DJ.

"Just so you know who is who: DJ, Mitch, Robbie, Matt." DJ continued on. "So, it will be the six of us taking off at our point day after tomorrow morning at 7 am," said DJ. "Tomorrow we do about 3 hours of training on the bikes," said Mitch.

"I am vouching for my brothers here…they will be quick learners."

"Then in the afternoon, you guys can see Charlie," said Sheriff. That brought a smile to all of the boys' faces!

Logan and Gage chatted with Robbie and Matt, giving them tips on the bikes. They made sure Bobby and Travis were in the loop since the deputies would be riding their bikes.

"We think this guy is there, laying low," said Sheriff. "But we expect that he is…and according to the doc we talked to, he said his finger bite was really nasty…so at least Charlie got him good! The doc was a little worried about giving out information about this guy…he didn't say anything to the doc, but he kept eyeballing doc, which freaked him out"!

"Oh, and by the way," said Sheriff. "This guy's name is Troy

Thompson, nickname the Snake"! The boys just looked at each other. Even his name sounded nasty!

The boys couldn't believe how bad this guy sounded! "You guys understand you are not to be anywhere close to these guys," said Jacob, looking straight at his boys.

"Yeah no worries, Dad," said Gage. "We get it. Not someone we're ready to mess with anytime soon!"

Next morning at 8:30 am, the boys were riding laps, along with Travis and Bobby. Mitch and DJ showed up with Robbie and Matt, unloaded their bikes and started riding laps. Mitch was getting to be a better rider very quickly. Robby and Matt got their riding gear on, and got ready to ride Travis and Bobby's bike.

"Hey Travis," said Robby. How about I ride your bike, and Bobby ride Travis's bike…that way we don't have Robby riding Bobby's bike. That would be too confusing." Everyone laughed and agreed. One thing about all the deputies…they were in great shape, and that made learning how to ride that much easier.

"Hey, guys, said Gage. "Watch how I stand, where I stand, sit where I sit, and the rest will come pretty easy. Have you guys ridden before?" Both Robby and Matt shook their heads yes as they put on their helmets.

"Yeah, we both actually had bikes many years before, so we'll probably pass Mitch and DJ in about 15 minutes of riding!"

All of these guys had become great friends in a very short period of time, and they totally respected Logan and Gage for their riding ability.

"Okay, follow me, and I'll follow Gage," said Logan. The Sheriff had shown up with Jacob to watch these guys ride, plus to give them new information. It seemed like the news of the day was never good news these days!

Both Robby and Matt were catching on quickly. Logan took the lead at the front, while Gage took got in line behind them. They stopped after a couple of laps, and Gage taught them a couple of things about going thru turns, and when to use the front brake primarily.

Gage did two hot laps with Logan, and Matt and Robby were blown away watching them! The good news is they were pretty close to being good enough to make it up to Silver Mines. The bad news, if they were rating this trail, it would be extremely difficult.

Trail riders rank trails from 1-10, with the easiest being a 1 (aka green), to a 10, being considered a black. This trail they are going to ride is a 9 or 10, in terms of difficulty! With very narrow sections and steep drop-offs on both sides of the trail.

Now it was time to head over to the woods, learn how to jump logs, how to go thru ravines, and a few other tricks that would help them on this trip. These trails are nothing in terms of difficulty they will face the next day, but…better than nothing!

Gage had one last trick to show off: a no-feet-over-the-log move, followed by a tight 4-foot turnaround using a front-wheel wheelie – then back over the log again. Only he and Logan had ever pulled it off clean. The rest of the group watched in awe.

The next morning came early 5 am sharp. The boys devoured huge breakfasts – lesson learned from past rides where they skipped food and regretted it later. Chloe came over to have breakfast with them, and was just hoping they would reconsider her being able to go.

"Grab your coat Chloe," said Margie. "You can ride with me, and then we will drive DJ's truck back over to where the Sheriff tells us to go. Then we come back home, and you will make it in time for school." It didn't make sense to Chloe yet, but she grabbed her coat just the same!

Jacob drove by the Sheriff station, all ready to pull out with the Deputies in their trucks. Bobby and Travis were there with DJ, they both lived closer than Gage and Logan.

Margie, the boys' mom, Margie, and Sheriff's wife, Susie, went along to drive both of the Deputies trucks, from the drop-off point to the end point. These are the kinds of things that were necessary in small towns, where the Sheriff's departments had small budgets. But, the entire trip was well-thought-out!

"Hey, guys," said DJ. "Let's not put on your warmest jacked yet," because we are going to work hard getting up to the top. THEN we will want our jackets on." The boys gave their mom and dad a quick hug. Logan and Chloe got a quick kiss, too.

"Gage, you lead," DJ called out.

"Logan, then Matt, Robbie you go next, then Mitch, and I will follow. Gage took off, standing on the pegs like he always does, and Logan, riding exactly like Gage. They didn't expect Robbie or Matt to ride like the boys, in fact, not even as good as Mitch or DJ. But they were holding their own.

They stopped at the bottom of the trail that would lead them almost to the top, and it was steep! Gage signaled to turn their bikes off.

"I say we get a drink of water here," said Gage. "Then, let me get up to that huge tree you see up there on the right. Then Logan will go up to same spot. We will be there to help if needed." DJ loved that idea, and he really liked the leadership these boys were taking in situations like this.

Both Gage and Logan made it up hassle free despite being single track and rocky. Matt went next, and was in the wrong gear. Thank god he changed gears with no problems, and remembered to keep his weight forward. Everyone made it up to this point without any problems.

The trail leveled off at this stopping point, then, dropped down to a small stream. The countryside was absolutely stunning up here! Off to the left were 4 or 5 deer watching these guys on the trail. Gage went thru the stream very methodically, very slowly, to keep dry. Everyone followed suit, except Robbie, who went thru it much faster, spraying water not only on himself, but Gage and Logan, who had gotten off in case anyone needed help.

As a result, his pants were now wet, but his boots stayed dry. This didn't make DJ happy, because he had already instructed everyone to ride as close to how Gage and Logan were showing the way! "Hey Robbie," said DJ, shrugging his shoulders. "C'mon dude, let's do what they do, okay"?

"Sorry," is all Robbie said. He was a good guy, but seemed to have a chip on his shoulder, which is the exact opposite of DJ and Mitch. Gage led them out again, and the same instructions applied when they got to the next big hill, which was slightly shorter…but also steeper.

They were now at about 8,000 feet, and on their way to 9,500 feet. There would definitely be snow at the top. In fact, they could see small areas near the top of the trail, which would be the next stopping point. It was definitely getting colder, but they were working hard to get up these 'Diamond Trails'.

As Gage powered up the incline, two large bobcats – watched from a distance. Beautiful creatures, but best left undisturbed. Matt stumbled getting up the hill, and Logan went down to grab the bike.

"Go ahead and walk up," said Logan. "I'll ride it for you."

He circled around Mitch and DJ, waited for a clear path, then tore up the hill on Bobby's bike—only his second time riding it, but he loved the extra torque. He powered through in a higher gear, flying up the slope with ease.

Now at the top, everyone put their next and last layer on; it was noticeably colder than at the bottom of the last hill. "I believe we are about a half mile from where the trail starts going down," said Mitch. "I've been on this trail, but never this far…keep a lookout for grizzlies and mountain lions."

"Hey the grizzlies shouldn't be awake," said Logan.

"Wanna bet," said Mitch, very confidently. "I have seen them at this time of year." Everyone was taking a drink of water before continuing on.

"We have one stream, or creek, coming up," said Mitch. "We go down about 1,000 feet before we see it, but it's coming up, and it will be very tough to get over"!

"How far to the hideout," Gage asked.

"You won't see it," Robby intervened.

"I know, just asking," Gage replied, unfazed. "Just curious."

Robbie's tone was sharp, and everyone noticed. Mitch gave him a subtle look—calm down, man.

DJ and Mitch exchanged glances. The tension wasn't lost on them either.

"Actually, I think you will be able to see it from the top of the trail," said Mitch, while he was eyeballing Robbie. He did it in a way as to say "hey chill dude," but he didn't say it out loud.

Both DJ and Mitch could sense this attitude Robbie was giving them. "All I can say is," said DJ, "thank god Gage and Logan are showing the way," also eyeballing Robbie!

Finally, the trail began to descend. Gage and Logan dropped in first, riding, 'Billy Bolt style', standing up, rear end back, knees bent. As it leveled off, they came up to the stream, and it was a fast-moving stream. They got off their bikes to look, and it was about 2.5 feet deep, about 6 to 7 feet across.

Worse, the banks on both sides had steep lips. Hit one wrong, and it could mean a crash and a flooded engine.

"I say we 'seat hop' it," said Gage to Logan.

"Agreed, but we should do it for Robbie and Matt," said Logan, as everyone was listening in. Everyone moved aside to let Gage go across.

"Hey Matt, Robbie," said DJ, "I think it would be a good idea to let these guys do it for you."

"No problem with me," said Matt. He parked his bike, and went up a small hill where he could jump across the rocks. "I got this," said Robbie, as he just stared straight ahead.

"Hey just the same, I'm responsible for everyone," said DJ.

"I'm not trying to be a hard ass here, just think it's the smart play, Robbie."

Gage got back, started off slow, then got his speed up, as he got to the front lip, he hit the throttle, wheeled and seat hopped across with ease, something he had seen superstars like Jett and Eli, Billy Bolt do before a hundred times.

Logan's turn, and he went across with no problems. They made it look simple. Gage and Logan parked their bikes, and went across the rock to get the other bikes across.

"Hey Robbie, get off the bike, dude," said DJ. "I'm not asking, I'm telling you…get off the damn bike." Robbie looked straight ahead, and finally got off the seat. "I know for a fact I could do it," said Robbie.

"Well, we aren't taking chances," said DJ.

"Hell, I have 5 times the experience you do, and I'm not doing it either, so let's chill the attitude, please, we have work to do."

DJ was getting irritated. Up to this point, he'd never had any issues with the moto boys, who ALL were better riders than Robbie. Clearly, Robbie didn't like someone giving him directions that wasn't his everyday boss.

Gage and Logan got all the bikes over with no problem. They still had some tough riding ahead. Going downhill was usually harder than going uphill. And the trail was becoming more difficult, because of icy areas. Lots of switchbacks.

Now they had a view of the valley below, and just a short area ahead, they'd see Snake's property. They had a few corners ahead that were challenging, that would require most of them to walk their bikes around the corner.

I'm Gage came across a big boulder in the trail, that for him and Logan, just meant lifting the front tire over the corner of the boulder, and making sure they didn't fall in the process.

Gage went over, as did Logan. They went up just far enough ahead and got off their bikes to help. Robbie didn't hesitate, he went for it! Unfortunately, he didn't plan this move out. He hit the corner of the bolder while accelerating, and his first wheel wedged in with the boulder and the trail. Robbie went over the bars, HARD!

The bike landed on top of him, and he yelled in pain!! ARRRGGGH, Robbie yelled. He was holding his arm. Everyone jumped off their bikes. "Holy shit," Robbie yelled, "I broke my arm." It immediately hit Robbie what his attitude cost him, as well as the group. "Crap," said Robbie. "I'm sorry, guys! "

DJ was careful to sit him up while holding his arm. His arm above his hand was very swollen, and even worse, very broken!

"Well, we'll let's deal with your broken arm right now," said DJ. "This looks like a pretty bad break. Guys, try to find me a fairly straight stick, and we'll wrap the hand and arm. Within a minute, Matt had found a stick that was suitable for Robbie's broken arm.

DJ, in addition to being an Army Ranger, was also a medic in the Army. He had Robbie's arm wrapped fast and tight in no time; he was clearly in pain! "Okay, you're gonna have to walk the best you can," said DJ. "You walk, and we'll each take turns getting your bike from section to section. You'll stay at the end of the trail with Gage and Logan."

DJ was irritated, but remained focused on the task at hand. DJ was clearly showing his leadership skills, as was Logan and Gage.

They finally reached the trail with the sharp drop. It was a tricky trail to walk down to Snake's property! They could see his backyard, and both Sheriff's trucks on the road in front, but probably a quarter mile from Snake's gate. "Sheriff come in," radioed DJ. "Come in DJ, how are you guys doing," said Sheriff. "We're ready when you guys say go."

DJ looked over his group, and saw that they were all off their bikes. Robbie was sitting down, bent over from the pain of his badly broken arm.

"We're now heading down," said DJ. "We had a situation, Robbie broke his arm, he's in a lot of pain but he's stable. He's staying up at the top with Logan and Gage. I'll give details later, but when we're done, he needs to catch an ambo to the hospital, and….he's gonna need surgery." Sheriff didn't say anything other than "Okay see you in a few, let me know when in position."

DJ kept his backpack on, but emptied out most of it to make it extremely light, as did Mitch and Matt. "See you boys soon," said DJ. "Let's go, it looks pretty steep going down. I'm putting in my earpiece, let's keep it stealth going down."

Now 4 pm, it took just seven minutes to reach the edge of Snakes property line. It felt amazing to DJ to finally be at this felon's house, the guy who almost killed Charlie! Mitch and Matt took their places, each hiding behind a tree.

It was extremely quiet. "Sheriff, we're in position," said DJ, quietly talking into his radio. Both Sheriff's walked up to Snake's front gate. There was no 'box' to talk into, but there were cameras, and he knew that if Snake was in the house, he could hear him.

"Open the gate Troy, we know you're in there," said Sheriff, very loudly. His two Rottweilers came running to the front gate, and they were barking loud….very loud! Both Sherifffs were well prepared; the last thing they planned on doing was harming Snake's dogs. Sheriff Don had his taser ready, and Sheriff Joe had his Stun gun ready.

And all the deputies had their Sig Sauer pistols in their holsters, as did the Sheriffs. No one was expecting a gun fight. That was the absolute last thing anyone wanted!

Sheriff started banging on the gate. "Troy, let's go, open the gate," said Sheriff Joe, this time a little louder. "DJ, move to your next position," said Sheriff Dalton, very quietly, and moved away from the front camera so no one could make out what he was saying.

Troy was pacing back and forth inside the house. Just minutes ago, he and the guys inside were drinking beer and playing pool, listening to loud rock music. "Hey Troy, maybe you make a run for it," said one of the other guys in the house, not yet identified. "It's just a matter of time before they make it in"ž

No one in the house called him Snake, they called him Troy, and they were definitely scared of him.

Troy kept pacing, and he was clearly pissed. "What are you guys gonna do," asked Snake. "You guys can't go with me, we can't leave the dogs. And I'm afraid you guys are gonna break! You will for sure, Luke."

Luke answered calmly but quickly to Snake. "Hey, I'm gonna say 'lawyer, lawyer', like we were taught, and so is Sammy." Snake looked at the TV's that had the cameras, and a couple of the views were even on the backyard. He grabbed his stash of money and keys, and went to the side door on the house.

This house was definitely older, but amazingly, it was pretty clean and well maintained. Inside the house, in addition to Luke and Sammy, were two women, sitting on the couch, not saying a word.

Yeah Troy, you need to get the hell outa here…now," exclaimed Sammy. Troy looked at everyone inside the house…and looked right into Sammy and Luke's eyeballs. "I'm not saying a word to anyone, you hear me," said Snake. "And I am not expecting you guys to be a snitch either, you feel me"!

He took one last look at every single person in the house. He grabbed his coat, and went to the side door. Before opening it, he looked up and down the side of the yard where he was going to exit.

"See you all very soon," said Snake. He quietly opened the side door, and made a run for the woods. "DJ, SNAKE'S MAKING A RUN," said Mitch! "LET'S GO," said DJ.

DJ and Mitch took off running for Troy 'Snake' Thompson! The Snake had about a 20-yard head start into the woods.

"TROY, STOP…SHERIFF'S OFFICE," yelled DJ, as both DJ and Mitch made a run for Snake. Snake was pretty fast, but DJ and Mitch were faster and in better shape!

"HERCULES…LUNA," yelled Snake for his Rottweilers, as he continued running. "STOP RUNNING TROY," yelled Mitch, as they were closing in, about 15 yards behind. But running in these woods was tricky, and Snake knew them much better than DJ and Mitch.

DJ and Mitch could hear the dogs coming fast. DJ made a lunge for Snake and tackled him to the ground. By now, Matt was also close behind. "MITCH, MATT," STUN GUNS," yelled DJ, holding Snake to the ground. Matt and Mitch formed a barrier for DJ so he could cuff Snake without getting bit by Snake's dogs.

"Just add another thing onto your list, Troy," said Troy, still out of breath from running. "Not too smart calling your dogs"!! DJ helped Snake up to his feet, after he was handcuffed. "Sheriff, we have Troy in custody, we're getting the dogs chained up now. We'll let you know when to come thru the gate," radioed DJ.

"Hercules, Luna, sit," said Snake, now trying to help his situation. "Thank you," said DJ. "We need them on a chain, will you help us with that," said Mitch.

"Sheriff, come in, dogs are controlled," said DJ. "Logan, you guys start down with bikes, and then we'll make trips up to get our bikes. How's Robbie doing." Logan and Gage got their gear on, and helped Robbie up with his good arm. He was in more pain, but somehow, he had to make it down the trail. It was not going to be an easy walk down!

"Robbie, you start down, we'll wait a bit before we start down," said Gage. "Hey I think you guys go first," said Robbie. Logan didn't say anything at first, but it made so much more sense for Robbie to go first, in case he fell or became unsteady. "Robbie, DJ left me in charge up here," said Logan. "It makes a LOT more sense for YOU to go first, in case you fall," so please…. will you just start walking"!

Robbie knew that if he tried to be an a-hole one more time, Logan was going to radio DJ, and it was not worth additional problems. He knew he was already in trouble with the Sheriff. "DJ, can you guys get an ambo here for when Robbie reaches the bottom," said DJ. "He's not in great shape."

There were a lot of moving parts now at the scene. Sheriff was getting ready to break the lock on the gate, when suddenly it started opening. Mitch and Matt had opened the slider from the back, and both Jimmy and Peter were there.

"We're all asking for a lawyer," said Sammy. "That's fine, said Mitch. "I saw you opening the front gate, so thank you for that. But right now, we're reading you your rights.

Logan and Gage waited about 5 minutes before they started down the extremely steep trail. It had switchbacks like the earlier trail, which made it just a little easier. They made it to Robbie in about two minutes. "Okay, we'll wait here while you keep going a bit," said Logan. "Robbie, are you drinking water," asked Gage. Robbie just nodded yes. He had a hard time with these two boys trying to give him any direction.

The boys and Robbie finally reached the bottom about 20 minutes later. By then, all of the people inside Snakes house were in handcuffs, and the deputies were going thru the house. They could not believe what they were finding inside the house!

"Okay Troy, we're taking you to the hospital first, to get your finger checked," said DJ. "Oh, and you could have said sorry to the young man you hurt, but he juuust checked out of the hospital"!

"I have no idea what you're talking about," said Snake. "Yeah, I bet you don't," said DJ, with a smile on his face.

Both Sheriffs were in Snake's house, as were an additional five deputies from Kalispell. The ambulance made it up the hill, and the paramedics helped Robbie into the back. "Hey hold up," said Sheriff Joe. "Robbie, I hear it's a bad break, it's going to need surgery, I'll check on you later today."

"Sheriff, it was my fault, I can't apologize enough," said Robbie. Sheriff smiled and said, "We'll talk about it later," said Sheriff Joe. "Right now, let's get that arm fixed."

In the back two bedrooms, three different tables were nicely organized with very expensive watches and jewelry. In the other bedroom, five cases of rifles and pistols were also organized, all of this no doubt stolen from the robberies in the county. "Get pictures of all of this first," said Sheriff Joe. "Then bag it, tag it, and let's bring it all in. Go thru the house, and if it looks valuable, bring it in, we'll sort it this next week."

It took about an hour for Logan, Gage and Matt to get back up the hill and bring the three other bikes down. They got everything loaded up, and couldn't wait to get over to the Diner for dinner. They were meeting with the other Moto Boys, including Charlie! He couldn't eat, but it was gonna be great to see him!

CHAPTER 16

We're Just Getting Started

The boys had a great time having dinner at the Diner with the other guys, including Charlie! Chloe was invited, and of course was sitting close to Logan. They were clearly boyfriend & girlfriend these days.

It was clear that the Moto Boys, at least Gage and Logan, had to be home schooled, because of their schedule helping the two Sheriffs. And it didn't look like it was going to change anytime soon!

DJ, Gage, Logan and Mitch made it up to Silver Mines in record time, and easily rounded up the trespassers, and had them all arrested by 3 pm the next day. Plus, they put two new cameras in operation, one in Silver Mines, the other over by the estates. There was still a lot of work to be done up there, because there were still at least four, maybe five, ways to reach Silver Mines.

Not surprisingly, Troy the Snake pleaded "not guilty," and asked for his lawyer. One of the other guys that were arrested, Sammy "Chains" Carter, had a bad rap sheet, and also pleaded "not guilty," and had the same lawyer as Snake.

The other man, Luke "Viper" Foster, and unlike the other two, was much younger, at the age of 24. He was in tears. He asked to talk to the Sheriff, and only the Sheriff!

"Hey, Sheriff, said Mitch, this kid wants to talk with you, but I want to be with you in the room, so I can learn from you. The Sheriff, looking over Luke's information, "Why not, let's go talk with him."

"Luke, I understand you want to talk with me," said Sheriff Joe. "I was hoping to talk with the other Sheriff," said Luke. Sheriff Joe thought about it for a minute, again looking at his information.

"Well, tell you what, Sheriff Walden will be here in about 15 minutes, and you can talk to all three of us," said Sheriff Joe. "You can take it or leave it young man."

Luke, still teary eyed and shaking, nodded yes to Sheriff Joe's response. Now out of the room, Sheriff Joe nodded to Mitch to move away from the door so he could talk without Luke hearing him. They walked by the rooms where Snake and Chains were being held, and they needed to be away from those rooms as well.

"I don't have a problem with him asking for Sheriff Don," said Sheriff Joe, "but I wonder what the connection will be…has me curious for sure."

Sheriff Don and DJ walked in about 20 minutes later, and met with Sheriff Joe and DJ. "Hey Don, one of the guys we rounded up," said Sheriff Joe, wants to talk with you. I told him we would wait, but he would get all of us. You okay with that?"

"I have a theory," said Sheriff Don. "Let's go in and talk to him…all of us!"

It looked intimidating to Luke, and that was intended. He still had tears running down his cheeks.

"Luke, I'm the Sheriff of Clear Springs," said Sheriff Don. "I understand you wanted to talk to me." Luke looked around the room with the other three who were in the room. "Can we talk alone," said Luke. "No," said Sheriff. "We want to help you, if you want to help us!"

"Okay, if I talk," said Luke quietly, "can you protect me"? Both Sheriff's looked at each other, and said "Yes, it doesn't mean you won't pay a price, "said Sheriff Don. But we know talking will help you a LOT more than not talking."

"But can you protect me," asked Luke. "I can tell you what you want to know…in fact need to know, but I need to know I'll be protected." Both Sheriff's walked out of the room for a second. "Actually, let me talk to him alone for a minute, Joe," said Sheriff Don. I think I can get a lot of info from this kid."

Sheriff Joe, Mitch and DJ went into the adjoining room with the one way mirror, grabbed a stool, their coffee, and listened to what Sheriff was going to learn about this kid.

"Sheriff, can you put in writing that I am going to be safe," said Luke. "If what I tell you, about what I know, and it gets back to Troy or Sammy, I'm a dead man"! Sheriff hesitated for a minute, and said, "let me ask you something Luke, is your dad the Chief of Police in Boise"?

Sheriff Joe, Mitch and DJ were hugely surprised, all looking at each other with mouths wide open. "What the hell," said DJ, quietly.

"Yes," said Luke, again with tears in his eyes. "Yeah, when I got on drugs, my dad was sick and tired of my crap," said Luke. "So, I moved out, I got a part time job in Billings, and found these guys. My dad did the right thing, and I realize it now. I was embarrassing my dad"!!

Sheriff didn't say a word at first. He kept staring at Luke. "So now you want to make it right," asked Sheriff. "Yes, in the worst way," said Luke. I'm sick and tired too, and I wanted a way out, but if I just left, I know for a fact they'd hurt me…probably worse.

"I want to see my dad, make things right, and get my life back…I prayed something like this would happen"!! Sheriff Don looked at Luke, stood up, and stood next to Luke. "Turns out your dad is one of my best friends, we've known each other for 15 years," said Sheriff Don.

Luke openly wept, he was both grateful and ashamed at the same time. He couldn't look the Sheriff in the eyes.

"I can't believe I let myself get in with gang," said Luke, wiping away tears. Sheriff Don put his hand on his shoulder. "Well, I'm gonna call your dad in a few minutes," said Sheriff Don. "Then I'm gonna come in with my guys," and we're going to get into some details, and IF, and I mean IF, we're going to help you…you have to help us, got it"??

Luke just shook his head, and nodded yes. He was still scared, knowing that Chains and Snake were next door. If they knew what was going on, he would do a lot worse to him, then they did to Charley.

Luke was the middle child, and although he had strayed from his family, deep down, he knew how much they all loved him.

Sheriff Don went into the room with Sheriff Joe, Mitch and DJ. "Well, you heard what I heard, I know Luke's dad," said the Sheriff. "Think about it, if we can get information that breaks up this crime spree, arrests these guys, PLUS get's the Russians that are these guys bosses…it would be worth getting this young man to cooperate"!

"Hey Barry, it's Don Walden, how are you and the family my friend," said Sheriff. "Hey I'm great, how are you and Mrs. doing," said Barry. Sheriff looked around at Sheriff Joe, DJ and Mitch standing outside, and waved them into the room. He wanted them to hear the conversation.

"I'm great, listen, this isn't a social call," said Sheriff. "We have your son here." Before Sheriff could continue, Chief Barry interrupted him, and said "oh crap, what has he done now. I tell you, he's not a bad kid, he just got in with the wrong crowd."

Chief Barry was trying to sell what he for sure thought was going to be a bad situation regarding Luke. "Hey wait Barry, just listen," said Sheriff. "Luke was in with the wrong group, and yeah, we have him…but he wants to make things right, and he wants to see you, and the whole family…when can you get here"?

Chief Barry didn't say a word, Sheriff could tell he was choked up. "It's 5 pm now, we'll be there by 10 am," said Chief Barry. "At least my wife and I will be there. Hey Don, if he gives you the info you need, can you move him down to a misdemeanor? I'm guessing there's gonna be charges"?

"If he gives us everything," said Sheriff Don, "I'm pretty sure he can go home with you tomorrow." Sheriff could hear his good friend Chief Barry get more choked up, at the idea he could have his son home with him tomorrow.

"Hey Joe," said Sheriff Don, "this Snake dude is going to figure out pretty quick that something's up when they don't see Luke in jail with him. We want to protect him as long as we can. But let's find out what Luke knows, and is he really going to spill the beans on these guys. But, not gonna lie, he needs protection"!

Both Sheriff's, DJ and Mitch walked in with Luke, all of them had note pads. "Okay Luke," said Sheriff Joe. "We expect you to tell us everything. Your mom and dad are coming over in the morning to see you. If you give us what we need, and it's good information, like really good information, then you might be going home with your family. If not, then we are going to hold you."

Luke was wide eyed, not saying a word, and kept nodding his head yes. He knew enough not to interrupt the Sheriff. "Absolutely, I'll tell you everything," said Luke. But...I'm scared of these guys, they know people, that know more bad people. But I want as far away from this crap as I can get, so I'll tell you everything I know."

Both Sheriff's started in, first asking questions about if was involved in hurting Charlie. "I had nothing to do with hurting him," said Luke.

"When Troy put the bag over his head, I told him not to do it. Ask the kid, he should remember me saying that. Troy told me to shut up, and quit telling him what to do. Then, the kid bit down on Troy's finger. Troy yelled at the top of his lungs, and that is when he started beating the living crap out of him."

Sheriff stopped him for a minute. "Okay, before you go on, what was the plan with putting a bag over Charlie's head," asked Sheriff Don. "I have no idea," said Luke. I'm serious…I have zero idea, we didn't get that far"!

"Why, Charlie," asked DJ, very direct and sounding mad. Luke looked around the room, and brought his voice down. "Because he just happened to be first," said Luke. "They didn't tell me who they were going after, or how, but I'm pretty sure they were going after all of the boys…the big boss was really mad about the guys showing up during their dinner at the big houses… or whatever they're called."

The big boss…that was information the Sheriffs couldn't wait to get!

Sheriff motioned for Luke to continue where he left off. "So…he was hitting him, and then stepped on the kids' ankle, I told him again… Troy stop!" He then reached over to slug me, but he missed. He reached over again, and got me right above the eye. He tried once more, but I blocked that punch."

Luke looked around the room for a second, and got emotional. "Then Troy opened the door, and kicked the kid out the door. I opened my door, to start to go over to Charlie. Troy and Sammy told me to get my ass back in the truck, or I would be next"!

"Okay Luke, I've got a question," said DJ. "First, he isn't called 'kid', his name is Charlie. Second, you guys stole Charlie's bike, yes"? Luke paused for a sec, "Well, I didn't, but Troy definitely did," said Luke.

"Troy told Sammy to pull over. And Sammy told Troy, 'I don't think we should, it's not smart'. But Troy just said 'I don't give a crap what you think, I said PULL OVER'! So…Sammy pulled over.

"Okay, so let me make sure we got this right," said Sheriff Joe. "Troy tells you guys to pull over, Sammy tells him no, and you tell him to stop hitting Charlie, and yet…Troy continues to beat the hell out of Charlie"??

"Yep, and after we left, Troy told us to find an urgent care, cause he was hurting so bad," said Luke. "But first, Troy being Troy, he wanted to go to a bar outside of town. He thought the alcohol would numb the pain. At the bar, Sammy started to talk to Troy, and told him Troy he needed to ditch the bike."

Luke hesitated for a second. "He really hurt that kid…sorry, I meant Charlie," said Luke. "And I think Troy realized that if the boss found out, they would really hurt Troy. He really screwed up…not the smartest tool in the shed!"

"Wait something isn't making sense to me," said Mitch, looking at DJ and the Sheriffs. "You say you wanted out…why didn't you just leave? After all, it's a free country."

Luke waited before he answered. He didn't want to be disrespectful, because to him, the answer was obvious. "I did, I told him I wanted out," said Luke. "But he told me, you know too much. You leave, and go run to daddy and tell him about us, you gonna have bigger problems with not only me, but the boss. I think it was someone named Max…this Russian guy"!

Sheriff Joe stepped in. "Okay, we're gonna get back to what you were telling us, but what does this Max guy have to do with you guys, and where in the hell IS this Max dude"!!

"I swear I don't know exactly where he's at," said Luke. "I met him once, and he didn't like me, I could tell." Now Sheriff Don came front and center to the table. To this point, he had been low-key and nice to Luke, because of his friendship with his dad.

But now he was getting frustrated, because he wanted answers…NOW!

"Luke, I want you to really think hard about what you're telling us," said Sheriff Don. Because IF the information is not good enough, and IF, it doesn't lead to these crimes stopping, then you're gonna go away for a long time…whether I know your Mom and Dad or not! GOT IT"??

Luke was still tearing up, and now he started crying again. "I swear, I'll tell you every single thing I know," said Luke.

"Luke, two more questions," said Sheriff Joe. Do you know who Dmitrius is, and do you know someone named Braxton"? Luke thought for a second. "Dmitrius I have never met, but I think I heard his name when Max came over," said Luke. "Braxton is another group like ours, well…theirs now, I'm not part of it now. He was a complete jerk, a lot like Troy, and had a nasty temper"!

"Let's step out for a sec," said Sheriff Don. "I want you to think about what we just said son"! Luke just looked up at the Sheriff, didn't say a word, and nodded yes.

As they stepped out of the room, Sheriff Joe realized they hadn't fed Luke. He motioned for one of the new deputies to come over. "Hey Lauren, can you get a dinner in there for Luke, please.

Listen guys, said Sheriff Joe. "I believe he's telling us the truth." And although I am ALWAYS the most skeptical guy on the planet, I think our best bet is treating him a little softer than we have...I don't want him to freeze up. I mean, he's answered every single thing, and if Troy or Sammy heard that stuff, he'd be in a ditch if we didn't protect him."

Another deputy came up to the two Sheriff's, and waited to make sure he wasn't interrupting. "Sheriff, I wanted you to know…we've been watching the monitors in the last half hour up at Silver Mines, and there is another group up there really riding hard and tearing it up"!

Both Sheriff's looked at each other, then at DJ and Mitch. "Shit, I swear," said Sheriff Don, shaking his head. "When it rains, it pours! Look, this whole project is is you two guys, and the Moto Boys"! "So, until we get the signs figured out and keep people out, you guys have to get up the mountain and feel with it"!! Both Sheriffs were exasperated and fed up with having to deal with sending these guys back up every week.

But DJ, Mitch, and SURELY the boys…all looked forward to going back up!! After all, it was their job! And it always ended in a dinner at the diner paid for by the Sheriff!

"One more thing," said Lauren the deputy. "Troy and Sammy are asking where Luke's at, and why isn't he in jail with them. He said 'something's up'"!! Sheriff Joe nodded and said thanks to Lauren for the information.

Again, the two Sheriffs realized the danger in Troy knowing that Luke could be snitching on the two of them! Even if they were still in jail, Troy had too many contacts on the outside, so they had to think about how Luke could be protected.

The Sheriffs and Deputies all filed back in to finish up with Luke, before his parents came in the am. "Well…why did Troy sell the bike he just stole," asked DJ. "That is a head scratcher for us."

"Sammy also told Troy that having a stolen bike in the truck could be a big big problem for him," said Luke. "Troy was focused on this finger. It was looking bad, and it really was hurting! So, Sammy found a guy inside the bar who wanted to buy it for $750. The guy knew it was stolen, but he had no idea just how it was stolen"!

DJ and Mitch kept looking at each other, kind of amazed… "So, Troy walks into the bar, has a beer, then suddenly, finds the guy inside the bar that wants to buy his bike," asked DJ. "Does that sound just a little weird to you Luke"?

Luke looked at DJ and Mitch, kind of shrugging his shoulders, "Yeah, I guess it does," said Luke. But I was on the outside of the conversation…not really listening until they went outside, and moved the bike over."

Luke was getting a vibe from DJ and Mitch, as if to say 'we don't believe a damn thing you're saying to us'.

"Hey I'm trying to tell you guys everything I know here," said Luke, a little exasperated.

"Okay, we're done for tonight," said Sheriff Don. "Luke, sorry, but you are still a suspect, so we have to lock you inside the room, we are bringing you in a bed, because we can't have you in the jail with Troy and Sammy. So, go do your bizness, and tomorrow am, when your parents are here, the questions will be continued."

Both Mitch and DJ had a lot more they wanted to ask. But they were exhausted and hungry. They wanted to fill in the boys, so off to the Diner they went, and met Logan and Gage.

The next morning, both DJ and Mitch were there by 9:15 at the Kalispell sheriff station. Luke's parents were in the lobby already, looking very anxious. Shortly after, Sheriff Don walked in, and immediately hugged Luke's parents, Chief Barry and Cindy. After they hugged, Sheriff introduced him to DJ, Mitch and then walked them over to Sheriff Joe's office.

"Hey guys," said Sheriff Don, "let me have a few minutes with Chief and his wife, and what they can expect. Sheriff looked at them, "I know you can't wait to see him," said Sheriff. Both the Chief and Cindy started to well up with tears. "Well, we never thought one of our kids would ever be in this situation," said Cindy.

The Sheriff stopped them. "Here's the good part," said Sheriff. "Yeah, he went down the wrong road, but he realized pretty quick he wanted out, and wanted to come home. But he chose some bad dudes to partner with, and then realized…he couldn't just get out whenever he wanted"!

Everyone stopped for a minute. "When can we see him," said Chief Barry. "In just a minute, you can. Because he was and is still a suspect, we have one hand cuffed to his bed. Give us a few minutes, let me get the room squared away, let him go to the bathroom, get him un-cuffed, and we can have you guys come in the room."

"Listen, we're not done asking him questions," said Sheriff. "We're gonna let you guys see him, then, you guys have to go out, and we finish. If we get what we need, then he can go home with you guys"!

Both Chief and his wife started crying again. "Okay," said Chief. "I'll let you get busy so we can see our son"! Sheriff excused himself to get Luke squared away.

"Hey Luke, your parents are here," said Sheriff. The deputy is going to take you to get squared away. We're doing a favor for your mom and dad. I'm going to let you get dressed in your clothes, but know this, the clothes from the jail can go back on quick if you don't give us every single answer we ask. We understand each other, yes"?

"Absolutely," said Luke. The Sheriff looked at him, tilting his head sideways. "Absolutely," said Sheriff. Luke wasn't sure what to say at first. "Absolutely, Sir," said Luke.

The Sheriff told one of the Deputies to get Luke taken care of, and to get his breakfast in the meeting room. "Sheriff, Sammy and Troy's attorney wants to have a word with you and Sheriff Joe," said Deputy Lauren. "Okay, take him to meeting room 3," said Sheriff. And I will tell Sheriff Joe."

"Let's get this meeting over with quick," said Sheriff Don. "I know this attorney, and he's a piece of work. Perfect fit for these guys"! No other Sheriff said another word, they just went to meeting room 3, opened the door, and were ready for business.

"Hello counselor," said Sheriff Don. "This is Sheriff Joe. What can we do for you." They all shook hands, and immediately sat down. "Hi Sheriff, it's great to meet you, my name is Richard Weinstein," said the Counselor. "I am licensed to practice law in both Montana, Idaho, and Washington. I have heard great things about what a tight ship you run here in Kalispell."

The attorney handed his business card to both Sheriffs. "I have a question, and a request," said the Attorney. "First, my clients will be pleading not guilty," said the Attorney. Both Sheriffs didn't say a word, they just kept their heads straight ahead, looking at the attorney.

"We understand you want to take them to county jail in Billings. Why there? Why not keep them in this jail"?

Sheriff Don didn't hesitate "Because he has a charge of kidnapping, PLUS attempted murder," said Sheriff. "And we typically don't keep offenders with these kind of charges in this jail."

Both Sheriff's knew that the judge and District Attorney in Billings, were much tougher than their own county.

"MURDER," asked the attorney, very upset. You're out of your mind, Sheriff! I'm sorry..but with all due respect, you HAVE to be kidding"!!

Sheriff kept his head straight ahead, just looking straight at the attorney. "Sheriff, you and I both know those charges won't stick," said the attorney. "We both know this Sheriff."

"Actually, you need to watch yourself counselor," said Sheriff Don! "We don't know anything of the sort." "You know what's ridiculous, you coming in here and trying to strong arm us"!!

Both Sheriffs were pissed! "You don't like it, take it up with the judge! If you are done, we have work to do," said Sheriff Don!

"I'll do that," said the attorney. "Hey one more thing," both Sheriff's looked at the attorney with a 'what now' look. "Luke Foster, I believe is his name?? My clients are telling me, that he's not in lock up with them, so he's probably trading his freedom, for giving false information about my clients"?!

"Are you for real," said Sheriff Joe. "I mean, if we did know anything, you think we'd tell you?" The attorney just smiled. "I believe you just did," said the attorney. "Have a great day"!

The attorney sounded slimy, and his questions made both the sheriffs feel uneasy. Both Sheriffs took their time answering his questions!

Luke was back in his clothes, pacing in the room, when the door opened. His dad was dad to him, not 'Chief Barry'. His mom already had tears in her eyes. "Dad," said Luke, as he gave his dad a huge hug. Both Luke and his dad had big tears in their eyes. "Mom," as he gave his mom the same huge hug.

"I'm so so sorry, for everything," said Luke, choking back tears. "Hey, right now son, give the Sheriff everything…and I mean everything, so you can get out of here," said Chief. "He's a man of his word…they both are, and it's the way you start to get this nightmare behind you"!

Luke gave his mom and dad one huge hug, and asked about his brother and sister. "Okay, let me get this nightmare behind me," said Luke. His mom and dad walked out of the room, as both Sheriffs, DJ and Mitch were about to go in. Luke could hear them all talking in the hallway.

"Hey Don, did you have any luck getting the other guys you arrested to get transferred to Billings," asked Chief Barry. Sheriff looked down the hall to make sure no one else was listening. "It's not looking like it," said Sheriff Don. "We talked to their attorney, and they said they will be staying here."

"But, we're gonna make sure Luke's not in danger," said Sheriff Joe. "He needs to tell us everything he knows, and we will keep Troy and his other guy's completely away from him.

The Sheriffs stopped to make sure it sunk in what they were saying. "Most likely Luke will be deposed to give info on this Troy and Sammy guy," said Sheriff Don, And that's where it can get a little dicey"!

Chief waved his arms. "Hey they can bring it," said Chief. Our team in Boise will be ready for those a-holes"! The Sheriff tried to calm Chief Barry. "Listen, I get it, but I'm telling you, it's complicated," said Sheriff. "It's involving at least two Russian bosses, and another biker group out of Billings, with the name Braxton"!

Chief turned to DJ and Mitch to shake their hands. "I want to thank you guys for helping me rescue our son," said Chief. I understand it was a really tough ride over the back way, and that one of the deputies broke his arm.

"Yeah, Robbie, one of our deputies here broke his arm," said Mitch. "He'll be fine, he just had surgery a couple of days ago, and he's home resting."

Luke had moved himself closer to the door to listen in. He remembered hearing that name 'Robbie' before, and that he was a deputy. He was trying to place exactly where he had heard this info.

"Good morning Luke," said Sheriff Joe, as everyone filed into the room. "Okay, let's get into the last questions," said Sheriff Don. First question, how did you pick these guys to be your hangout gang? I know you've been asked this before, but why did you pick them? Why these guys"?

"I was in Billings, and I started doing coke," said Luke. "I was an idiot, partying, riding my Harley, bouncing around at a few friends' houses. I ran into Troy and Sammy at this bar in Billings, and we started playing pool. They started asking questions about who and where I was sleeping. And I needed a place to sleep and hang out. At least I thought I did."

Luke stopped for a minute to catch his breath. He was super nervous all over again! "They told me they had a nice house way back in the hills that was gated, and that I was welcome there for a bit. So, I took them up on it. I never asked what they were doing"!

"You never thought to ask them what they did for a living," asked Sheriff Don. "I mean, that seems like a pretty simple question, right?" Luke thought about what he was going to say next. "I agree Sheriff," Luke said. "I don't think they would have told me the truth, knowing what I know now," said Luke.

"Okay, Max is the guy everyone is afraid of, is that right," asked Sheriff Joe. "Yes sir, like I said, I only saw him one time," said Luke. "I tried introducing myself, but he ignored me. I asked who he was, and what did he do. Sammy said 'You ask too many questions', so…I quit asking."

The Sheriffs and Deputies were taking notes, when Luke spoke up. "If I was to guess, he must live close to Billings, because he got to the house in less than 20 minutes from the time they spoke on the phone."

Luke paused while they wrote notes before continuing. "I know this…Sammy and Troy are not the only ones involved in the crime deals, they're about 3 to 4 groups," said Luke. "And Braxton is just one of them."

"And the thing I'd worry about, is… this Max guy was really mad about these boys interrupting his dinner that night. He escaped, and he was really mad at Don and Larry for not being more careful"!

"Max wanted to get back at the boys…but apparently, he's really mad at Troy for being so reckless, and taking a chance at hurting that kid! I do know this …I would help you guys any way I could to get these guys, because hurting Charlie…was just plain wrong, and it was stupid"!

There was silence in the room. "One last thing," said Luke. "I overheard when Max was there, him saying to Troy, that they had someone on the inside. He didn't elaborate, but I would guess it was a District Attorney or a judge"?

Nobody was saying a word. Finally, Sheriff Don said, "Okay Luke, we're going to go out and talk. If we let you go, are you really willing to go to court and testify when we need it"?

Luke didn't hesitate. "Yes, yes, and yes," said Luke. "If I can possibly make my dad proud of me after what I did, I will do anything to help. And I am a very good motocross rider, if that helps"!

"I have one more question guys," said Luke. "One sec, Luke, Mitch, and I will be right there," said DJ. Mitch didn't know what DJ was gonna ask, but both he and DJ sat across from Luke, lowering their voices.

"Luke, who are the brothers Larry and Bob?" said Luke. "Oh, those guys," said Luke. "They met Troy one night at a bar is Kalispell. We all sat down, Troy bought them beers. Larry started talking about how they had an inside in Clear Springs at being able to rob houses. I think it was his aunt."

Both DJ and Mitch looked at each other. "Like what kind of inside," said Mitch. "Not sure," said Luke. I was thinking they were casing people's homes. Plus, it was their idea on hiding stolen stuff up at the ghost town."

Both DJ and Mitch filed out and went down the hall with the Sheriffs, so that Luke could not hear them. "This is NOT the first time I've heard this," said Sheriff Joe that someone with the DA's office, or possibly a judge, could be on the take in our county"!!

"This cannot leave this circle," said Sheriff Joe. "Not even Robbie, who did the ride with you guys. We have huge problems ahead with this Max guy, and now, we may have a leak on the inside"!

Sheriff Don looked at the four of them. "Let's get to work, and figure this out. It sounds cliché, but…our towns are counting on us"!

Both Sheriffs, DJ, and Mitch went into say goodbye to Luke. No doubt, it felt good to see the Police Chief get his son back. As the Chief, his wife, and Luke were walking outside, Troy and Sammy's attorney was there, watching them walk to their car. The Chief knew who the attorney was, and how him seeing his son drive off with his dad…well, was putting Luke in danger!

DJ, Mitch, and the Moto Boys were going to be busy, to try and preserve Silver Mines and the Haunted Estates, plus helping the Sheriff get Max. Hopefully, Troy would pay for what he did to Charlie!

DJ and the Sheriff met the boys at the diner, later that night for dinner. They filled them in with what had happened. The Sheriff also told them how important all of the boys had become to the town of Clear Springs, and for their help, both Gage & Logan were both getting two brand new bikes! Two Yamaha Tenere 700 Rally bikes!

Gage and Logan were very familiar with these bikes, and they just looked at each other, wide eyed, in complete surprise! Jacob, their dad, already knew about the surprise, and all he could do is laugh when he saw the look on their faces.

Now all of the boys had new bikes except Charlie, but in spite of his bike being stolen, it was still working and riding really well. "Charlie, you'll be next, we appreciate you so much," said Sheriff Don.

When the boys drove home that night, they felt so proud for being a part of something that helped their town. They realized how important they all were to their community! Once upon a time, some of the kids in town were heckling the boys, but in reality…they were more jealous that they couldn't do what these boys could do!

But Gage and Logan also knew…they were just getting started!

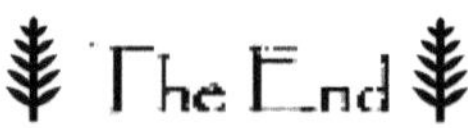
The End

9 781969 506345